Brothers

Mary Ann Peck

Four brothers are using trades between their companies to manipulate the economies of countries where their companies are located. They are threatened with exposure if they do not use their abilities to fight terrorism throughout the world.

They soon learn that terrorism is controlled by two methods.

Author: Mary Ann Peck
Authored the following:
"Inside-Outside"
"Grand Arriba"
"Welcome Home Susan Canby"

Contributor: Russell C. Arslan
Authored the following:
"Those People"
"Highest Stakes, All In"
"Leopard Directive"

Mary Ann Peck

To order additional copies of this book, contact:

PeckPublishing.org
orders@peckpublishing.org
Call Peck Publishing at 404-801-4010

DEDICATION

Dedicated to my four sons:

Walter Leroy Peck

Gordon Hathaway Peck, Jr.

Jimmy Eugene Peck

Thomas Alexander Peck

The Peck brothers are as different

as the characters in my book.

ACKNOWLEDGMENTS

Thank you TomG, who gave me the greatest gift a writer receives, he critiqued my manuscript.

My gratitude goes to all my friends who read and criticized the early versions and especially Ida Acunto, Erika Clethen, Rose Marie Durocher, Bonnie Gavazzo, Teri Grey, Elaine Haber, Donna Hoch, Margie Marsh, Patsy Myers, Don Mills, Juanita Montana, Sam Taybi, Robert Weinstein, Heather Wynters and my grandson Cody Peck who listened to bits and pieces of the story with encouragement.

Special thanks goes to Russell C. Arslan whose encouragement and technical contribution is immeasurable, but most of all thanks for being my friend.

Brothers

CHAPTER 1
TERRORIST ATTACK

Marko Fushier walked down the colonnade between Harvard's historic ivy covered buildings. He was scheduled to teach an economics class at 9:30, but this tall slender, curly haired professor was not hurried. He wore tight blue jeans, a white shirt with a blue sport coat and strolled along enjoying the spring sunshine while thinking of his life. He had accomplished his dream of a Doctorate in Economics, specifically Input-Output theory. He had recently received tenure. He knew his parents would want to know right away. As a permanent Harvard Economics professor, he was very pleased and proud. He knew his parents would be also.

Today he was enjoying the new leaves on the old elm trees and the birds out there singing to each other. He said to himself, "This will be a spectacular year."

As he approached the Student Union Newsstand his eyes suddenly riveted to the headlines: "TERRORISTS KIDNAP U.S. AMBASSADOR AND OTHERS." He thought his heart would stop.

Marko grabbed the paper, threw down money on the counter and started reading the article while he walked.

"During a reception in Argentina, Supremenistas stormed into the American Embassy. The U.S. Ambassador, the German Ambassador and the Secretariat de Estada De Paraguay were forced to leave with ten armed men and additional guards at the doors. The U.S. Ambassador's wife ran through the terrorists to her husband's side, demanding they allow her to go instead, she said, "My husband is ill. He will not live through the night without his medicine. Please, I will go."

With tears running down his cheeks, Marko read to the end of the article skimming over reactions from German and Paraguayan Embassies and the impact these terrorists' acts made on the world at large.

The people these newspapers talked about so carelessly were his mother and father. His beautiful mother so calm and understanding, so devoted to his dynamic father, whose high blood pressure kept him from doing many activities.

The guerrillas had escorted her upstairs. While she collected her husband's medicine she snatched up some clothes jamming everything into a gym bag. When they came back to the main ballroom, she grabbed her husband's arm and wouldn't let go. The Supremenistas didn't have time to argue and took her with the Ambassador. Marko shook his head and thought, "That's just like her."

She loved her tall, handsome Frenchman with all

her heart. He was so attentive and ultra-romantic, always telling her how beautiful she looked even though they were in their nineties now. His mother and father had been in their late forties when Marko was born. He thought all parents were gray haired, not that his mother ever had gray hair. Her hair was bright red always. She said, "That's the color I was born with and that's the color I will die with, Irish red."

His father would hug her and laugh when she said that. Marko still didn't know why they thought it was funny. He assumed it was one of those lover expectations fulfilled. They always told him, "We've had a good life. We've been blessed with a son we never thought would happen and a life of living all over the world. We've experienced ten different nations working as ambassador."

Marko was raised as an *embassy brat*. He went to elementary school in France, and Japan. Later he schooled in Turkey, Spain and Italy. When it came time for college he wanted to attend one school the whole time without moving and always being known as the new kid. His grandmother, Maggie Scot, lived in San Francisco so he went to Berkeley to be near her. She was going on one-hundred at that time, spoke with an Irish brogue, said funny Irish things Marko's understanding not grasping the full meaning. She never told him exactly how old she was. He was always glad he had time with her before she passed away. After he graduated Berkeley, he enrolled at UCLA and still went up to visit her on weekends, but she told him one day, "I won't be here much longer. You are well on your way now, *Sonny*. I have other things to do so don't grieve for me when I'm gone. I want a big Irish wake, a celebration."

Within two weeks she passed away. She always called him *Sonny* and loved him more than he could ever return. He never understood the strange look she gave him when they met after some time had passed. He thought all grandmothers did that. She left him saddened by his loss. Now he was losing his mother and father also. He wouldn't let that happen without a fight.

He started walking. In a daze, he deliberated the possibilities, thinking, "What can I do?"

Then he remembered his old friend, Doug Henry. Marko met the ex-treasury agent and kept in touch after going on a Montana climbing expedition where the mountaineers ran into an archeology group digging dinosaur bones.

Marko took out his pad and started making notes while talking to himself, "First, I'll call Doug Henry, then the CIA, Sofia at the State Department and anyone else who might help rescue father and mother in Argentina. Oh! And I'll have to take a leave of absence from teaching, a month should be enough, but I'll ask for the rest of the semester off."

Students were walking along talking on cell phones, discussing plans and subjects during their break in classes. As Marko walked through the campus talking, he didn't seem the least bit out of the ordinary.

Marko continued, "The real help will come from Doug Henry. That's where I'll start."

Doug had been an agent twenty-five years before he killed one of the people he was investigating and never quite recovered, so he retired, went to Chile with his pension and now spent all his time searching for antiquities.

"If anyone can find mom and dad, Doug can. He spends his time roaming around in strange out of the way places. He'll go places nobody else even knows exists."

The first call had been to Doug's home in California. The message said, "Gone south, looking for very old bodies. Call back if you're over 200 years old."

Marko called *the office*. After identifying himself, he was told to come with three forms of ID to be checked before they could give any information concerning Mr. Henry.

On the midnight flight to Washington, DC, Marko was thinking about the story Doug Henry told him reminiscing one night, sitting beside a dwindling fire. Doug started saying, "I am a man at peace with his past."

Continuing he told his story. It hadn't been that way when he first arrived at the archeological dig. He had come here to grieve. Grief that sits there gnawing in your stomach. It was like sitting in a cheap hotel, hearing the scamper of vermin in the walls. There's a rat gnawing on the base board of the room upstairs and as you listen, suddenly the realization comes. The gnawing in your stomach pulsates with the rhythm of the rat upstairs.

He kept remembering over and over the slow motion movement after the gun was fired. The clawing and catching only air, the scream that came out more like a gurgle as the blood rushed through his lungs drowning him. Then the blood oozing at first then flowing from his nose, his mouth and finally his ears. Grief carried with him every day had begun to subside. He couldn't bear to remember without being sick now, but at first the grief sat there gnawing in his stomach like rats.

The Doug Henry who sat in the sleazy hotel would then vomit until he only dry heaved over the slop bucket by his bed. He stayed holed up like that for six months reliving that boy's death several times a day fearing himself, but fearing the outside world even more. Finally *the office* made him go see the boy's family. One of the Marys, Fred always haired a secretary named Mary-something, made all the arrangements. Fred Hoskin's office or rather his secretary, Mary Rose, called to set it up. No one was sure what Doug would do but, they thought they had to try. Doug Henry represented an investment to the Treasury Dept. Henry had killed before. Seven people. He had read in a report once that of all American males over age 18, 51.25% have deliberately killed another human being in their lifetime. In Desert Storm Doug Henry had been decorated for killing but that was different. Those were people who looked different, spoke a different language. When he got home he knocked around awhile – When a guy says, "I knocked around," it just means he didn't work steady. Finally, Doug got a roster of government jobs and there was this job – <u>Agent Trainee</u> bookkeeping and accounting, foreign language preferred, interesting job with travel as auditor, expenses, per diem and salary paid.

Doug took the preliminary test and must have scored high because Fred Hoskins's secretary, then her name was Mary Gwen, called all peppy and gushy asking to set up an immediate appointment.

"Your test score indicates you are prime Treasury Agent material."

Doug felt rather like she had called him a beef steak. He understood now that she had. Their investment kept Fred Hoskins and his secretary Mary Jo from writing him off back in '98 when he surprised the Maddock Brothers at the Tucson Airport and in the shoot-out following Doug killed Ron Maddock. Doug got six weeks leave, went to his apartment on Zuma beach, played in the sun, saw the shrink they assigned and went back to work. However, it wasn't as simple with the boy at the brick yard. It was his fifth *line of duty* and it took longer for Fred Hoskins and his secretary, Mary-Something, to recoup the losses.

When he signed on, Doug had gone to college three years at Treasury's expense, one year at the University of Mexico, studying African sociological changes, after two at Berkeley studying Chinese, later he had a few months at the University of Oslo studying French.

Doug Henry was the Treasury's 'third world' expert. Somewhere in the midst of all those languages and history and cultures Doug discovered what he really wanted to do. He liked detail. He liked mystery. He liked to hunt for the solution. But he found archeology was much more to his liking than chasing criminals for the Department. After over 25 years in the Treasury he wasn't convinced they really were all criminals.

He was taken to the Stadler home and expected to see the parents of the boy he killed. Mary Jo made all the arrangements and Doug Henry went along, hoping to receive some kind of redemption or understanding of his actions.

Doug walked up the Stadler front entrance. A stout bug-eyed man stood behind the screen door. Doug knew Stadler had watched even as they drove within view, parked and got out of the car. It was Monroe who went in with Doug. He was glad it wasn't the other one. Monroe was just prissy and fat. The other agent driving was heartless and one of the two truly mean people Doug had ever known.

Mr. Stadler opened the screen put out his hand and said, "Mr. Henry?"

Doug nodded, "Yes."

They all looked through each other as if not to see the person would make it easier.

Harold Stadler motioned Doug to an armchair and sat himself in a straight back kitchen chair.

Marie Stadler came into the room. Doug and Monroe jumped to their feet, she just stared straight ahead.

Harold Stadler said, "Marie, bring the coffee."

She went to the kitchen and brought a tray she had prepared. There were four cups of instant coffee, a sugar bowl, two spoons, four napkins and a pitcher with milk. Without asking she gave Doug and Monroe their coffee, put milk and sugar in one for her husband and took her own black.

Doug just stared at the Stadler's not believing these two hard working people who raised that kid, sacrificed their money, maybe even their health to give that kid a better advantage than they had, could sit there blandly drinking coffee with the murderer of their son.

Mr. Stadler broke the silence, "I understand you are grieved over the killing of Richard."

Doug had to fight to control the horror again. As he sat there he could feel the rat gnaw his stomach and knew only too well the next sequence. He could not allow himself to get sick in these people's living room. He fought the ache in his belly. He drank a swallow of the black coffee. It washed away the rat momentarily.

Mr. Stadler was continuing his slow drawl, "We know Richard was no good. A mother always loves'em. I guess even a mother snake loves her young. But we don't blame you. We know you was only the instrument what did it. If it hadn't a been you it'd a been another."

Doug Henry stared at this couple, "Thank you, Stadler, for saying that, but it's not you I'm asking to forgive me. I have to forgive myself before it's alright."

And as Doug Henry stared at these old bitter people he knew. He had given himself the answer. He had not found it at the Iroquois Hotel vomiting in the dark, or wandering in the dark city streets.

Henry abruptly rose and shook Mr. Stadler's hand turned to Marie Stadler and said, "I'm sorry." And hurried out the door, leaving Monroe fumbling with his coat and knocking over the coffee cup then sopping it up with his clean white handkerchief and rushing after Doug Henry who was back in the car with Alfred the surly driver.

"Alfred, take me to Fred Hoskins's office."

Monroe jumped into the back seat and hissed, "You stupid fool, now you've done it. They'll sue for sure. What ever you've got in your head, go back in there and apologize, you fool. You're not going to do this to me."

"I didn't realize I was doing anything to you."

"Don't you think you could at least be civil? You murdered their son."

When Monroe had said murdered the rat got lose again gnawing vehemently, and as the pain shot through his lungs, Doug vomited all over Monroe's well groomed lap.

Monroe screamed, "Oh, my Gawd, Alfred, Stop! He's – augh, augh."

And then Monroe was vomiting out the window.

Alfred slammed on the brakes turned half way around and slapped Monroe across the face and grabbed for Doug screaming, "You Bastards, you filthy bastards."

Doug jumped out the door when the car stopped.

Alfred drove the car into a driveway, walked over turned on the garden hose, drug it to the car, pulled Monroe out and proceeded to hose him off. Very little throw-up remained in the car since Monroe had gotten the brunt of Doug's upheaval. The three men stood glaring at each other.

Finally Doug said, "Alright, now will you take me to Fred Hoskins's office, Alfred? That is if Monroe can keep his trap shut."

The three mechanically got into the car and drove to the office without speaking.

Doug Henry marched into Fred Hoskins's office with Mary Rose chasing him saying, "Stop, you must be announced."

"Doug, you're back so soon. I thought you would have a nice chat with the Stadlers." Fred Hoskins cooed as if trying to sooth an irritated child.

"Fred Hoskins, I am retiring. Have Mary Rose, or Mary Jo or whatever Mary she is draw up the papers for me to sign. Now. I won't be in the U.S. tomorrow."

Fred Hoskins looked at him steadily measuring everything, calculating the investment, then turned without answering and spoke into the intercom.

"Mary Rose, come in with your pad and the standard voluntary retirement forms."

Doug quietly continued talking very deliberately. He knew his future, perhaps his whole life hung on his next few words.

"You have to give me a disability retirement. I would be no good to you vomiting every time someone mentioned uh, that word."

Fred Hoskins replied smiling his official smile, "Yes, I know. I've known for some time. I just hoped you could be salvaged."

Fred Hoskins looked worried. Doug thought he was wondering exactly what word would set off the spewing, maybe, salvaged?

Mary Rose quickly brought in the proper form filled out correctly and it all proceeded without a hitch.

Doug said to Marko at the end of his tale, "When I thought about it later, I wondered, if she already had the forms filled in."

The next morning Marko appeared at Fred Hoskin's office. Marko was greeted gushingly and of course they already knew who he was and why he wanted to see Henry.

"You're that kid who visited with him in Montana when he was digging there. I thought you sounded familiar."

"Yes, sir," answered Marko.

Fred dropped his eyes and said, "So very sorry to hear about your folks."

"Thank you," Marko answered. "That's why I'm here. I plan to go to South America and look for them."

"Son, I wouldn't advise that."

"I can't just sit here and wonder."

"Well, son, we have all the agencies working on it 24/7 and you can't do more than that now, can you?"

Finally Hoskins agreed to help. "Okay, okay, here. It's a map showing approximately where he may be. It's all I can do except suggest you get assistance in the village, Sacra."

"Thank you, Mr. Hoskins. Anything you can do to help me speed up the search is appreciated."

Hoskins said, "I'll arrange an escort to accompany you from La Paz, Bolivia," explaining, "Henry's in Chile or Bolivia about 300 miles from Ixiamas but he's high up in the Andes, and he digs every day. If you're lucky you might find someone who delivers supplies to him. We've sent up three orders since he's been there this time. The area is in the Andes cornering Chile, Peru, Bolivia, and Brazil."

Everything became a haze of action after that. Marko took a leave of absence from the university. In two days the army flew him to La Paz. An operative met Marko there and put him on the Andes express train going to Sacra. Finally Marko made it to Henry's cabin and talked him into helping find his missing mother and father.

Marko and Doug searched for four months. They were tired, weary of the trekking and finding nothing. They were high in the mountains when a Quechuas Indian approached their vehicle. He motioned to Doug who recognized him as the Chief's son. He said, "You look for the Americans?"

"Yes, this is their son. He is mourning their disappearance. Do you know anything?"

The Quechuas Indians living in the most isolated Peruvian mountain area were distrustful of any government entity, but they talked to Doug Henry. Several years ago he had done an archeological dig which found their relatives' mementos. Doug had petitioned the government and the area was set aside as a commemorative region, honoring their ancestors. The Chief refused to deal with the government, but was always helpful when Doug came around the area.

The Chief's son answered, "My father has something to show you. Please come with me to the camp."

Marko and Doug were hoping they had found the ambassador and his wife. They went to the Chief's home. The Chief brought them back to the camp area, showed them two graves and said, "The Americans were left with the doctor who takes care of our people. The Americans were very old, but still trying to keep going. After three days here, they died of *the fever*. They were buried as one of our ancestors."

CHAPTER 2
MARKO CONTEMPLATES

Marko grieved for days at the grave site, but finally Doug said, "Come on, I have to go home and check on things. You need to come with me, until you get over this."

The State Department people wanted to move the bodies to Arlington, but Marko refused. He simply accepted these graves as his mother and father's end. They were together and would never be separated. He never dug up their remains nor would he allow the State Department to do so. He was very tired, weary from searching. He went with Doug to his home in Chile. Doug said he should stay until he recuperated from the searching and his parent's death. It was mid-winter in the Andes, cold with snow and storms.

Marko had his correspondence, books, newspapers, magazines, supplies and laptop shipped from his Harvard office. All mail accumulated over the last six months was sent. In this remote mountain aerie he began reading. He started to compare notes and study the discs containing Input-Output system calculations sent from his Harvard office.

Trying to become part of the world again, he read the magazines and newspapers accumulated in his office during his absence. His attention was gradually drawn to several large multinational corporations. At first glance, it appeared the groups were making purchases independently. After further observation and application of the Input-Output equations, Marko realized the conglomerate with Amsterdam home offices' buys and sells meshed with another company. He discovered the companies were making very organized decisions and thus controlled specific commodity prices on the world's market.

They had not stockpiled or illegally monopolized any one commodity, but like a trout fisherman gently playing the lure, a whole pool of trout had jumped to the bait. Invariably other companies bought what another group had in surplus and what at one point looked like ruination of the steel industry turned into all the supporting companies following the bait right along to make more business for all in the consortium.

After his attention was drawn, Marko studied in depth the history and buy/sell ratios of the two companies and eventually came to a conclusion. It wasn't just two, but five corporate entities successfully manipulating the world economy.

During his research, Marko discovered Chung Kee Lee, Farimo Abba, Constantine Kaulas were each children of Vernon Velgrove. Marko had started a spreadsheet and kept adding companies and countries as he gained more knowledge about the Velgroves. That spreadsheet showed all the raw materials produced by their companies and all the finished products manufactured with the available natural resources. This spreadsheet, called Input-Output Analysis was designed by Wassily Leontief who was awarded the 1973 Nobel Prize in Economics for that macroeconomic system.

The one strange piece not quite fitting their operations was the New York office being managed by a holding company *until other arrangements can be made.* What other arrangements? Why was it on hold? Marko searched every place possible, but his information was limited while stuck there in Chile. Therefore, he said goodbye to Doug Henry and his wife, Nissa, Doug's handyman, Romero and his family. Doug made sure Marko had the equipment secured on the donkey and had Romero accompany Marko down the mountain.

Marko was welcomed in his Harvard office. The January semester had just begun. Marko spent weeks getting back into his routine. Riding his bicycle to the office daily, organizing his shelves again, counseling students and researching the Velgroves. In actuality he found very little further information, but he couldn't give up the idea of avenging his mother and father's deaths. He was sitting there searching yet another dead-end when he looked at his desk calendar and saw the date. One year -- the day they were abducted was today.

At his desk Marko sat, staring at the wall. After awhile he started typing and by midnight he had finished demands outlined in a letter he would deliver to the Velgrove International Industries, NY, Inc.

Attention: Chung Kee Lee: After studying the actions of the five Velgrove companies and testing the structured interactions with Input-Output analysis I have prepared the following documents showing your latest economic manipulations and have distributed several copies to my friends and acquaintances to be used in case of my demise. I am prepared to publish worldwide accounts and reports to criminal investigators. I make one demand. To stop the public humiliation of your companies you must employ your vast influence and tremendous power to stop terrorism throughout the world.

He continued assembling sixty pages of data compiled about the companies. He worked on the document until 4:00am. Marko rushed to the airport, managed to obtain a ticket for the first New York flight, took a cab to the Velgrove Industries office on Broome Street, walked in and demanded to see Chung Kee Lee.

The receptionist very politely explained, "Mr. Lee is in Hong Kong, sir. If you have information for him as you say, I can send the letter in our night mail. He will have it tomorrow."

Marko replied, "Is that the only way to get it to him?"

She nodded, "Yes, sir."

"I guess it will work, one more day won't make a difference. What is your name?"

"My name is Rosalyn," as she fluttered her eyes. She wasn't really flirting, just making the conversation interesting.

He handed her the envelope, said, "Thank you," and left.

CHAPTER 3
BROTHERS THREATENED

Chung Kee Lee, the oldest son of Vernon Velgrove, received the communiqué with interest. He had known it was possible, even probable, someone would figure out the cooperating companies' existence and the applications they were using to *gently guide* the world economic conditions. Okay, manipulate if you will be brutal, the results of many world situations. But here it was in full view and at a very inconvenient time since so many circumstances were in flux right now.

Chung was eighty-six, owned fifteen software companies and six computer component manufacturers in six different countries. With over 26% of his company's assets invested in Computer Software and another 10% in Computer Hardware, the other brothers cautioned Chung that he was over extended in the computer industry, but he stuck to the belief that the world was running on computers now and he had to stay in the middle of it to keep his company stable.

His father, Vernon Velgrove, had started in mining, gas and oil. All the Velgrove companies continued to keep that strong base. Medical would always be needed and clothing manufacturing was historically Asian so that left his business diversification to management industries, travel, insurance, media, shipping and storage.

Vernon Velgrove had returned to Hong Kong in 1945 when his oldest son was twenty years old. Chung Kee Lee knew his half Chinese and half Caucasian background was the reason his mother sent him to Catholic schools. His father took him to the U.S., Chung never regretted it. He was educated and groomed to run Velgrove Industries. When Chung made some money he invested in Hong Kong companies. His father made him feel loved and part of the Velgrove family. He met his three brothers and they learned to work together.

Now this upstart was trying to ruin their lives. If the Velgrove brothers did not meet with the blackmailer and form a plan to cure the terrorist problem, Marko Fushier threatened to make public the five Velgrove companies' economic manipulation. His notification to Chung Kee Lee started a fireball of action.

Chung Kee Lee assembled the most trusted employees in his Hong Kong boardroom. Chung gave instructions to research immediately into the remotest details of Marko Cogburn Fushier. "Who is this person who has the audacity to threaten us?"

Chung had little information about Marko Cogburn Fushier. What kind of crazy name was that? Marko could be Spanish, Cogburn could be German or something and then Fushier, definitely French. No wonder the poor man was so confused.

Chung would get more information about the man, but this threat called for a conference of all the brothers together. Not one or two, but all had to make this decision. If the aggressor carried out his threatened exposure, it would destabilize the whole Velgrove multinational group affecting their future business outcome in fifty-three diversely different countries and maybe reaching further. This threat to make public their identities as half brothers and sons of Vernon Velgrove, if they didn't form a mercenary army wiping out all terrorism, would be just the beginning of trouble. Once threats were carried out there would be more coming.

Marko Fushier wanted the Velgrove companies to solve the world terrorism problems. In his letter he envisioned a crack troupe of mercenaries who could march into any country and put down an uprising. He had seen how the companies controlled political leaders' selection and even ones they didn't approve they often used a politician's idiosyncrasies to manage the economic future of that country.

He had cited the election of Governor André Puccinelli of Mato Grosso do Sol and Governor Silval da Cunha Barbosa of Mato Grosso, two western Brazilian states bordering on Bolivia and Paraguay. The Velgrove companies had requested these governors stop the shipment of FMD (Foot and Mouth Disease) virus coming across state lines in vehicles. Products and by-products were designated as health risks and refusal of agricultural products originating in Paraguay or from slaughterhouses without refrigerators were banned at the state line. It was considered the most economically devastating livestock disease in the world.

The governors cooperated and closed the borders with decrees to the Mato Grosso neighboring states of Rondônia, Amazonas, Pará, Tocantins, Goiás and Mato Grosso do Sul where border crossings were monitored for the disease.

Marko Fushier had made pages and pages of spread sheets showing interaction of the products sold and bought by the Velgrove companies. These numbers were interesting to Chung but he didn't have time to study it and dissect the meaning.

The Velgroves had dealt with attacks before. He remembered the incident with Connie and Garland. Both had been physically attacked. He also knew realistically, all terrorism would never be eliminated.

It's even impossible to define terrorism. There is neither an academic nor international legal definition of the word 'terrorism.' Various legal systems and government agencies use different definitions of terrorism. The international community, United Nations or World Bank have not universally agreed on a legally binding definition of this crime. The difficulties arise because the term terrorism, systematic use of violence and intimidation to achieve a goal is politically and emotionally charged. It is common for violent conflict opponents to describe the other side as terrorists. Terrorism has been described as *the dirtiest weapon of the weak against the strong.*

In his letter to the Velgrove Group, "Terrorism is so prevalent," Marko stated, "couldn't someone make an impact on these weak renegades who want to rule the world one bomb at a time?"

As Chung stared at the document he said to himself, "Sure they could, but lack of organization makes it impossible to even try."

Marko wanted a one year time limit set for formation of the military group. He had information of black ops performed by Army rangers, Navy seals and others. Why not form a Corps Velgrove, hiring the same soldiers to go in and stop the terrorists' actions before they happen? Most countries would welcome help from a Special Forces Unit in emergencies threatening their governments to subdue groups planning terrorist operations and using wars or the threat of war as an international manipulation vehicle.

Another side to terrorism, the recently exposed Shabab Militia, who seized families' crops and livestock then imposed taxes making it almost impossible to survive according to a report released by Human Rights Watch, accused the Militia banned international humanitarian agencies as 'infidels' and told the desperate population to depend on God instead. The impact of Al Shabab's total prohibitions on food aid in areas under its control was devastating. Somalian refugees fled to Kenya. The Al Shabab attacked international humanitarian organizations, accusing them of pursuing religious or ideological motives. Theft and blockage of food had exacerbated starvation in an already tense drought affecting an increasingly resource scarce environment. Many refugees were not allowed to cross the border to obtain food.

There are many forms of violent attacks. During the last weeks, attacks in Iraq targeted solders, police officers and market shoppers in Najaf, Kut, Baghdad, Baqubah and other areas. Ali Haidari, a security expert, said the assaults came shortly after Abu Mohammed Adnani was named Al Qaeda's new leader in Iraq. The terrorist group had been announcing on its website for weeks the preparation of a major operation to exploit the Iraqi forces perceived weakness.

These differences did not make it any less devastating to the people targeted. The use of the Input-Output system to analyze economic well-being of the terrorist areas would lead to better methods of determining and controlling the disparate causes of peoples involved.

Marko had ended his terrorist dissertation with: *if only a few fiends are stopped, the world will be a better place.*

Chung was beginning to get reports from his staff. He soon found Marko's father had been an ambassador to Argentina. Marko was a Harvard Business School Doctor of Economics. He had three classes and an office in one of the most prestigious universities in the world. He had prestige, money, an education and future in his profession, why did this person think he could manipulate the Velgrove Group into illegal activities?

The remains of the Ambassador and his wife were found in South America. The State Department had moved in to test the remains, but Marko refused, permitting no interference. He arranged for a local merchant to lay a new wreath on their grave once a month as long as Marko could not be there.

Chung Kee Lee understood how losing your mother and father could prompt desires to dispose of all those responsible. Chung reasoned if something similar had happened to Vernon Velgrove and his mother, Ling Mei Su, he would have tried some retribution. He understood the young man needed to avenge the death of his mother and father by wiping out terrorist acts, but did not understand blackmailing the Velgrove's.

Delving into Marko Fushier's background, Chung identified with Marko's desire to honor his family. Chung's father would have been similarly honored had the same thing happened. However, no matter what this person believed, terrorism had been around since the word terrorism was first used as *government intimidation during the Reign of Terror in France* and derives from French *Terrorisme*. In a speech Robespierre delivered to the French National Convention, 1794, "If the basis of a popular government in peacetime is virtue, its basis in a time of revolution is virtue and terror -- virtue, without which terror would be barbaric; and terror, without which virtue would be impotent."

Chung was a Chinese businessman respected by his family and community. His son, Sun Fo Lee had businesses of his own in Shanghai and along the

Wangpoo River. When the ninety-nine year British Hong Kong Lease terminated, Chung was very active in negotiations to keep Hong Kong as the Chinese outlet to the world. Chung and his family had been sitting on the edge of the world for over a hundred years. They had coordinated the British within the Chinese territory and the Chinese trying to make business with the rest of the world. Until Chung had been found by Vernon Velgrove, he was a half Caucasian outcast. His mother had hidden him from other Chinese family members when he was young. After his father came and took the young man to be educated and trained in business, he returned as a hero who owned his own business and was coordinating products and industries with other businesses in the outside world. He was forever grateful that his father had been a man of loyalties.

Chung Kee Lee instructed his assistant, "Follow the trail of Marko Fushier's family background."

After only a few minutes on Google she found the American Ambassador to Argentina information, it took hours to establish who the other members of his family were. His mother, Eileen Scott Fushier and father, Reni Olivier Fushier, had affluent backgrounds. Reni Fushier's father and mother were both French immigrants to the US in 1935. Albert and Ellie Fushier established French fashion in New Jersey and sent their son to college where he met Eileen Scott at Oxford in 1945. The Fushiers had one son, Marko.

When the assistant presented her report to Chung Kee Lee, she apologized for not finding pertinent information about the person who was threatening Velgrove Industries. "I did not find any indications of crimes."

Chung said, "Let me see what you did find."

As Chung read the report he could not believe his eyes. He immediately called his assistant. "Find who are the mother and father of Eileen Scott. Did her mother attend Oxford in 1915?"

After a few minutes the assistant came back, "Sir, you are amazing, how did you know those details?"

Chung laughed, "The man we spent over a million dollars trying to locate has found us. The son of Eileen, daughter of Maggie Cogburn, only a small jump in imagination confirmed he was the grandson of Vernon Velgrove. That long lost Maggie Cogburn has been found at last."

Vernon had always been sorry he didn't marry Maggie when he had the chance. He called it the worst mistake in his life, but proceeded to modify that statement with, "If I had married her I would not have had four wonderful boys or maybe they would have had a good Irish mother. Thank you boys, I appreciate the good you have done and all you have given me."

Chung was totally stunned. He stared at the report for ten minutes, "This ablolutely changes the situation, completely!"

The shock of finding her after ninety-five years of looking, first by Vernon Velgrove searching sixty-six years for Maggie Cogburn before he died in 1980 at age ninety. Then each brother, Chung, Farimo, Connie and

Garland, spent their time and money investigating. As Connie had said, "Nobody can just disappear off the face of the earth now, can they?"

CHAPTER 4
MEET MARKO

Chung picked up the phone and dialed his brother, "Connie, you will never believe what has happened. I will be in Los Angeles in fourteen hours. Please notify Garland and Farimo. We must all meet. My daughter Mei-Ling will also be there and Vernon Velgrove's grandson, Marko Fushier will be the honored guest."

"What in the world are you talking about?"

"Just as I said, you heard it. It is difficult to believe, no?"

"How did this happen?"

"It seems we were all looking in the wrong direction. When I ran a search on the fellow who is blackmailing us, I found he is the son of Eileen Scott Fushier, who is the daughter of Maggie Cogburn Scott. How about those apples?"

"Chung, if you say it's so, I have to believe it. So he found us."

"It would appear. We still must check the DNA."

"Too much depends on this. He is the heir to Velgrove Industries, NY? Have you told Charlie?"

"That's right, Connie. Sun-Fo will have to handle this, won't he? He will come to realize he already has a fortune and does not need more. I need you to arrange the boat in San Pedro for our meeting. I want all four brothers aboard the boat to decide these procedures. Vernon Velgrove would be so proud this young one has found us."

"Wouldn't he be astonished? I'll take care of the details as usual. Don't worry, I'll get them there. Do you need me to talk to Charlie?"

"No I will tell him. Nancy will be there but I will handle that arrangement. I'm asking her to sit with Mr. Fushier at the San Diego Yacht Club while we arrive from San Pedro. At UCLA I will check on her facilities, things you can only see in person. I get there so seldom, this will give me a chance."

"Chung, what date shall I set this meeting?"

"Two days from now, Saturday, your time. It will probably take until evening to assemble at the boat allowing for flights and appointments."

"I will get to work on it. It's still amazing, don't you think?"

"Yes, it's very amazing, Constantine."

When Chung notified his son, Sun-Fo Lee, who was in New York managing the necessary details there he didn't expect the outburst he received, "Sun-Fo, we have an occurrence here. We are being threatened by the Grandson of Vernon Velgrove. He threatens to expose our company interactions. We will have a meeting in Los Angeles next week. I thought you should know."

"Pop, how could you let this happen?"

"Well, Sun-Fo, it has happened. The long lost grandson of Maggie Cogburn and Vernon Velgrove seems to have found us."

"This is terrible. I lose everything. Don't you see father? I would have been first to assume the Velgrove Industries, NY CEO. He has taken my inheritance. How could you let this happen? Why didn't you call me? I would have taken care of this idiot?"

"My son, we are reputable people we do not 'take care of people'. You are never to talk to anyone about this subject again. You must never mention this to anyone."

Chung listened while his son slammed down the phone. This would not be easy for Sun-Fo to accept. He had made big plans for taking over both the Hong Kong business when his father stepped aside, and the New York office when allowed. It would have been soon according to Sun-Fo. Chung was concerned, but he had many arrangements to make for the brothers' meeting. Chung hung up and started buzzing his assistants to assemble in the meeting room.

Chung addressed his most important company people. He presented information, brought forth facts about Marko, the man making threats to Velgrove Industries, revealing that the grandson of Maggie Cogburn and Vernon Velgrove had indeed been found, explained he would be in Los Angeles meeting all the family partners to decide what changes should be made.

Vernon Velgrove had searched sixty years for Maggie Cogburn. In a blink of an eye, her grandson had found them. Vernon would have been so proud of this young man. It took guts to challenge the whole world and its terrorist ways. Chung knew his brothers would have similar feelings but they needed to express them in their own way. Chung Kee Lee would propose they take Marko into the corporation and family.

Chung thought about the solutions to their problems during the long flight to Los Angeles and finally emerged with a plan to question Marko about the practical applications of his Input-Output System studies as a ploy for time. Marko needs to become a full fledged Velgrove and shoulder the responsibilities of his decisions. We will give Marko the problem assembling the Corps and what attacks are made.

Thus, the family meeting was set into motion.

Meanwhile, in New York Sun-Fo or Charlie as he was known to his buddies was not taking the news easily. He called three friends to meet him at the local bar. He left his office and approached the front door. Seeing Rosalyn he stopped and asked, "Hey Chickie, what do you know about a letter we received yesterday that was sent to my father?"

"Yes sir, I received that and put it in the overnight to Hong Kong."

"Next time just give it to me, Chickie."

"Oh, sir, I would lose my job for that. Every letter must be delivered to the addressee, you know, Federal Offense."

"I run this office. I will open all mail for this office." He slammed his fist on the desk and left.

Raymond and Joe were waiting for Charlie when he walked into the bar and said, "I can't believe the bullshit of office employees. Why can't somebody do something right?"

Raymond and Joe looked at each other wide eyed. Joe, the bravest of the pair, said, "What did I do now?"

Charlie answered, "Oh, don't be stupid. You didn't do anything."

Raymond added, "This time."

The waitress brought their order and they sipped their drinks. Charlie continued, "Some fool has appeared from out of nowhere, claiming he is my grandfather's heir."

Both Joe and Raymond said, "What the......?"

Joe added, "You were just about to take over the whole thing. How can you let this happen? We'll all fight for you, you know that, right?"

Charlie answered, "Let's figure out a plan of action."

Jonathan slid into the booth and asked, "Couldn't get loose from that bitch up there, what did I miss?"

"Nothing much, Charlie's just lost his inheritance," Joe said facetiously.

"O-M-G! What's going on?" Jonathan exclaimed.

They all looked at Charlie. "Well some guy is blackmailing the old boys. They're having a meeting, but you know how they react. Like Christmas coming in July."

"O-M-G! Blackmailing?" asked Jonathan.

Joe said, "Would you stop that *text* talk, Jonathan?"

Raymond added, "Yeah, dude, that's old hat."

"Hey, what kind of blackmailing? What are they threatening?" asked Joe.

"I don't have all the answers, I just want to get my team together, you know, you guys." Charlie answered. "What do you say Raymond? What can we do?"

Raymond had been sitting there quietly observing. Finally he said, "What a you gonna do? Take out a contract on the guy?"

Charlie nodded his head, "Just what I was thinking. Who knows anyone in that field?"

Joe chimed in, "We need to research this. You don't just jump into a situation like this," he lowered his voice, "or the next thing you know you'll be in jail."

Charlie jumped to his feet screaming, "I don't want to hear that. Get the fuck outa my sight."

Joe slowly rose and walked out the door.

Raymond looked at Charlie and Jonathan, "Charlie, you gotta get a grip. We're all here for you. If you think about the situation, you'll understand what Joe's saying."

Charlie yelled at the waitress, "Give me another drink."

Raymond was the calmest of the group. He had known Charlie for twenty years or more. They had been in school together. Charlie's father had given Raymond karate lessons when Charlie took them after seeing Jackie Chan movies. Charlie started dressing like J. Chan as he called him. He didn't run up walls like Jackie but could take care of himself. Raymond became a black belt fifth level. Charlie was only a first level black belt. They were schooled in Hong Kong and then went to Stamford in California. Charlie's father asked

Raymond for assistance many times. Raymond was sure Chung would not make the same mistakes Charlie did. Raymond and Charlie's father had an unspoken agreement that Raymond should not report on Charlie, but, "If possible keep Charlie out of trouble."

As Charlie and Jonathan talked animatedly about who they could hire to wipe-out the blackmailer, Raymond thought about all the ways to solve this without harming Charlie or the business.

CHAPTER 5
BROTHERS ARRIVE

At LAX, Los Angeles International Airport, Garland Posey Velgrove, a six feet five Texan, managed to duck through the car rental booth line to the beautiful redhead on the end. She glanced up once then turned half around as she recognized the broad toothy smile. He carried a bag and was dressed all western, cowboy boots and all.

"Hi, Daddy, how's your trip?"

He flashed the Velgrove smile again as he answered, "A little touch 'n go there, darlin', but I convinced 'em I could make it through those ol' clouds. How're you doin' Jacqueline."

"I was concerned you wouldn't make it in tonight," as she stood looking professional as she pushed the paper work across the counter for his signature.

"Well, guess you can just go ahead with your plans, I'm gonna haf'ta drive a long way tonight. The fog's tied up this whole coast."

A definite frown briefly clouded her otherwise happy face as she said, "But you'll be back. When do you pick up your plane?"

"Monday, maybe Tuesday, as I see it now. Hang loose, Darling, I'll see you then."

He grabbed the papers and kissed his daughter before running toward the car lot where he slowed and started to limp. Garland Posey allowed his mind to drift as he walked the hundred yards to the cars parked for drive-away customers. He enjoyed flying his own plane, driving himself. He enjoyed it because then he never had to explain where he'd been or where he might be going.

But the real reason was Garland had a limo driver a few years back who had connived to make extra money by setting-up his boss. The driver was late. Knowing Garland would be in a hurry and take the car and drive himself. Half way to the airport a car ran in front of his Cadillac and was T-boned. The occupants of the car hit the floor before the collision and were injured only slightly. They sued for millions and would have won, but Garland got out of the hospital after three weeks and came home where he saw the car's driver talking to the limo driver. An investigator was able to prove the limo driver and the people in the accident were all working for some ambulance chasing lawyers. After that incident, Garland decided he could drive himself better and faster than waiting on some outside guy who would just screw up his life. Since the accident, his broken leg had given him pain. However, right now he was going to a meeting of the brothers. He had not seen all three together in over ten years.

Constantine sounded so mysterious. Of course,

Connie had a penchant for the melodramatic anyway. But somehow Garland had believed the urgency, the hurried stillness of his tone when Connie said, "We must meet. Chung Lee has made the decision that we must decide this among ourselves. We can't just pull strings on this one."

"Connie, you know we agreed never to see each other all together, it's really better that way, don't you think?"

"Oh, of course, it's always worked but we cannot avoid this question any longer."

Connie had always been the go between. He was the perfection of nonchalance. The non-sequitur in the median, he floated from one country to the other. He was a film-maker. Truthfully he could do any job handed to him. But it was his escapades that really paid off. The media was always ready to print the *facts* of his latest soiree with Lady Jill, or Princess Fara or the star of his latest smash hit.

He wintered in the Alps, summered in Wales and did his stint in almost every country of the world. There were no boundaries not seen by his passport during the last ten years. And just when the press had him safely confined to the Prince of Wales' villa he would suddenly turn up with his best cameraman and footage obviously taken at the head waters of the Amazon or other equally exotic locations.

Only lately had Connie begun to settle down. His new wife and baby made a big difference in his life. He had stopped the wild trips and parties in Europe. He still turned-up any place they asked him to go, but he rushed to return home. Garland knew his brother Connie better than the other two because they had grown up together in Texas.

After Connie finished college and went to Europe for awhile, Garland was living on the ranch and Connie came to live there until he recovered from an injury suffered while filming a race at Le Mans. Connie had always been Garland's older brother and taught him the ways of the world, but they still fought like brothers often do.

Garland squinted through the fog at the freeway lights. He was glad the traffic was moseying along slowly. He moved onto the Harbor Freeway and headed for San Pedro. In about twenty minutes he was inching along when suddenly he came out of the fog at the peak of the Vincent Thomas Bridge going on to Terminal Island. Directly in front of his rental car he was rushing into the rear of a parked car. He had to swerve to avoid crashing into it. As he passed he saw no one in it and uttered an obscenity about irresponsibility. Looking in the mirror he shook his head, but pieces of Volkswagen suddenly rushed past him. He hadn't really seen a blast but his ears rang from the compression and the impact knocked his car several feet into the oncoming bridge lanes. He corrected sharply and hit the accelerator. The windshield cracked as some debris hit the right corner.

Garland Posey did not stop nor look back but sped on through the foggy black night. Slowly a dank, gnawing foreboding sank over the usually smiling Texan. As he drove, he wondered if the other brothers were already on the boat or would they hit this same blown car. Garland dialed Connie's phone, "Connie there's a wreck on the bridge leading to the dock. Watch yourself."

"Don't worry; I'm waiting for Farimo outside the theatre. Oh, gotta go. I think I see him now."

After leaving his office, Constantine Koulas had walked the tree covered street with dampness dripping all around. It was not actually raining; the trees dripped a cold bone-chilling wet. He tried not to appear hurried but before he had gone three blocks his teeth had set-up a chatter that would put a monkey's cage to shame. "That's the trouble with Los Angeles weather," he thought to himself.

"You get so accustomed to the good weather, when a foggy night like this comes along it throws you for a loop." As he approached the corner he could see a dark car hesitate and then stop under the light in the next block.

People started to surge forward out of a theatre down the street to the left. Constantine turned right and stepped into the dark alleyway. The black car sped to where he waited, stopped briefly while he slid into the warm back seat and rubbed his hands and face to start circulation.

The driver's black face looked at Constantine in the mirror and gave him a big toothy Velgrove grin. Connie returned the smile and nodded as the car picked up speed along Figueroa Street where they turned into the entrance marked Harbor freeway south. Farimo Abba glanced at his watch and nodded to Constantine as their eyes met in the mirror of the black limo. Farimo said, "Nice to see you, my brother."

Connie rubbed his hands and stated, "You'll never believe what's happening. We're facing the toughest decision since Vernon died."

"It seems so long. I know he would have loved this kid who has the guts to challenge us."

"Yeah, you can bet on that. Who told you the details?"

Farimo continued, "I've been having some other troubles, and called Chung, he filled me in on the find."

"Can you believe how much damn money we wasted trying to find that kid and, he literally walks into the front office in New York."

"Is that where he dropped off the threat?"

Connie answered, "Yeah, what a deal. We need to watch Charlie's reaction. You know he was ready to take over the New York office. He won't take this lying down."

"Yeah, he said he was looking forward to taking over last time I was there," Farimo dodged debris on the bridge, "We should call that in to the police. I wonder what happened."

"Garland called on the cell and told me there had been a wreck. I should have mentioned it when I got in the car. I'll call in a report when we reach the boat." Connie answered.

Farimo guided the big car off the ramp onto the side street and in a matter of minutes was stopped in front of the slip next to the fishing boats. Farimo got out, opened the back door for Constantine and escorted him to the gang plank where he boarded the three-masted schooner.

Two Chinese sailors appeared from the fishing boat vicinity and came aboard the REGAL SONJIA. A tall longshoreman walked from a near-by restaurant sauntered down the walk, took the keys from Farimo and drove the car away. As Farimo walked on to the boat, the two Chinese sailors disconnected dock lines and the graceful boat slowly glided out of the slip toward the harbor entrance.

The Coast Guard Boat saw a blip moving on their radar and started for the harbor entrance as the REGAL SONJIA moved out to the open sea.

"Hey, Ron, It's just those SONJIA guys again."

"Yeah"

"It's the third time this week they've been out at this time."

"One'a them told me the other night at Stanhoe's they're adjusting a new radar."

"Well, if it's not working tonight, they're in lotsa trouble, it's thicker than vichyssoise out there."

"Yeah, well I think they like it in the rough weather. Last Thursday they took it out in that blow."

"Two'o them guys sailed her around the cape last year in chubasco season."

"How many was in their crew?"

"I think it was Hi Shu and Sam Luk."

"Man I guess if they took it around the cape, this stuff we got tonight seems like child's play."

"Sure, but I'd hate to have to go to Catalina tonight for a rescue."

"Yeah. Invariably some a-hole will come barreling along like he's the only fool in the world."

"Those guys have spent their whole life on the water, I guess."

"Yeah, you know what Luk said one night in Stanhoe's? Them guys over in Hong Kong are born on a junk, live all their life on one, and when they die....well, I don't know. Maybe they drop'em under it for the fishes."

"Looks like they made it through the narrows, let's go back up to the Charthouse."

The REGAL SONJIA was a one hundred foot, steel hulled, three masted schooner built in Amsterdam. It was captained by Shu. First mate, Wu Kee, was Shu's nephew, Luk served as navigator and general logistician. The crew varied from one time to the next, depending on family activities. Shu and Luk's sons were all experienced seamen. Any one of them could have sailed around the world alone with no trouble at all. The sons were aboard when they weren't in school. Both fathers were determined their sons would be educated sailors.

The schooner was leased to agencies doing ocean surveys and Wu Kee and Luk were well known to the oceanographers at NOAA's Center for Operational

Oceanographic Products and Services. They recently worked on the East Coast El Niño effect.

When Chung was discussing their new boat, he asked why they were going to the east coast. Shu explained to Chung Kee Lee the reason for considering the offer to use the REGAL SONJIA in the studies. Shu answered, "El Niño is a weather phenomenon most people associate with the West Coast characterized by unusually warm ocean temperatures in the Equatorial Pacific that normally peak during the *cool season* (October to April) in the Northern Hemisphere. El Niños occur every three to five years, with especially strong events occurring about once a decade. El Niños have important consequences for global weather patterns, often causing wetter than average conditions and cooler than normal temperatures across much of the central and southern United States,"

Prompted by the highly active El Niño of 2009-10, they reviewed 50 years of data on cool-season water levels and storm surges at four east coast sites: Boston, Massachusetts; Atlantic City, New Jersey; Norfolk, Virginia; and Charleston, South Carolina. A storm surge defined as a rise in coastal sea level of one foot or greater has been occurring more than usual. The report, released by NOAA, in partnership with the U.S. Census Bureau and U.S. Environmental Protection Agency, provided economic and ecological highlights about the east coast communities', economy, and ecosystems. The sailors on REGAL SONJIA had worked with government agencies so much they were automatically given choice jobs when new studies were considered.

The brothers used information gathered by the REGAL SONJIA when not leased to the government. Their fishing crews off the west coast of South America were known for their knowledge of the fishing areas and regional weather changes.

Even in their educations the sons gravitated toward the sea. Hi Shu was a marine biologist who spent vacations, leaves and project times on the REGAL SONJIA. Len Kei was a cartographer of high merit and one of Sam Luk's sons was an oceanographer consulted by oil companies before opening the field in the north seas. He was first to discover the possibilities of oil in the Indian Ocean field years ago.

Next summer they would join the NOAA Ship FAIRWEATHER, A 231-foot survey vessel temporarily stationed in Kodiak, Alaska on a mission to conduct hydrographic surveys in remote areas of the Arctic where depths have not been measured since before the U.S. bought Alaska in 1867. NOAA will use the data to update nautical charts helping mariners safely navigate this important but sparsely charted region, which is now seeing increased vessel traffic because of the significant loss of Arctic sea ice.

The Velgrove brothers planned to buy a larger ship with more up to date equipment. The boat was a good investment, since so much time of the boat, crew and equipment was being leased to the government. The Velgroves were able to use the boat this weekend before it left for Alaska and its work there.

CHAPTER 6
MEETING ON THE BOAT

Nancy Chang leaned against the railing at San Diego Yacht Club staring into the fog. In spite of her confidence, there was a strange feeling of approaching doom nagging at her confidence. Her brother Charlie had called before she left the university, asking questions. Why did he have to be so belligerent? He could be nice when he wanted. But more and more he just yelled at her when he called. She had learned to keep the conversations on the lite side and never talk about business. Pop didn't know how screwed up Charlie could be.

Pop always said, "Mei-Ling, little one, your voice of doom does not coincide with your lovely name which means 'butterfly'."

"Pop, maybe I'd be better named *moth*. The moth knows he only has a span of time before becoming a worm again."

They would laugh together, but tonight standing there alone, staring into the murky fog she didn't feel like even a smile. She kept asking herself, "Why? Why did these gentle men work so ferociously to go pummeling out to sea on a night like this? What could be so important?"

Yesterday she had been in her dormitory room dreaming of Kenneth Wong, her chemistry lab partner when the day mistress called up from downstairs and informed her, "Miss Lee, your father is waiting to see you."

Nancy flew down the stairs and hugged her father and gave a little yip as he swung her around. Then as the staid Chinese exterior overcame the excitement of the moment they both bowed and her father calmly said, "And how is my daughter progressing in this school?"

"Father, I just made the dean's list."

"What significance does this list have?"

"Oh, the highest grade points in the school are honored. I was not the highest; I still have trouble in Qualitative Chem. This semester I have the cutest guy as a lab partner and he's so smart. I have to convince him of my diligence by making higher grades."

"It is not enough to make higher grades for your father?"

"Oh daddy! You already know how smart I am," as she gave him a quick kiss on the cheek.

In spite of himself, Chung Kee Lee gave a quick glance around to see if anyone had observed. He knew kissing in public was acceptable in America but it still made him feel nervous.

"Father, why are you here?"

"I have business and expect you to join me on the boat tomorrow night. It is necessary to make some very important family decisions and you should know how these contemplations proceeded in years to come when you have a more responsible role in our business."

"That sounds ominous."

"Perhaps. You should be at the San Diego Yacht Club no later that 10:00 A.M. tomorrow morning. Do you need any help arranging this? We could be gone several days."

"No, father. We're having semester break and I'm only getting a head start on my next classes. In ten days the new classes start."

"Good. I thought the timing might be such."

Mei-Ling knew her father kept hundreds of schedules in his mind and hers were always accurate. This was not the first time he had suddenly appeared during one of the school breaks to broaden her education. They had been to last year's Space and Aeronautics conference in Zurich. Her father had sent her to the National Wildlife Counsel meeting two years ago as an observer. With the stipulation she would write a full report for her botany class and his business.

Her father continued, "You will meet Marko Fushier there. You must stay with him until we arrive with the boat. He is a dilemma to the family business. I'm trusting you to handle this as a family member."

Mei-Ling was astonished at the seriousness her father just expressed, "Father, I will treat this assignment with the utmost expectation."

"My daughter, please stay as close as possible with Marko. You will meet him in the yacht club and wait for the REGAL SONJIA to arrive. At that time you will come aboard with him and we will immediately head out to sea again. I am meeting all the other brothers tonight in San Pedro where we keep the boat and will immediately go to sea. The brothers will have a meeting and then we will meet with Marko tomorrow. You have a reservation at the San Diego Hilton for tonight."

Mei-Ling stopped by San Diego Yacht Club that evening to do a walk through. She had supper and left for the Hilton. She was prepared for the next day.

CHAPTER 7
BROTHERS MEETING

As the boat sailed into darkness, the brothers gathered in the library. Drinks and snacks were served. Tonight the thick fog and the moonless sky's darkness made traveling eerie and gloomy. While, the brothers were assembled to discuss problems of great importance, the gloom gathered outside.

Each of the four men sat in the lounge taking in the countenance of his other brothers. They had not spent time together in years. How could it be? They instinctively knew the others and how they thought. They talked on the phone many times each month, but the actual looking into each distinctively different face and all its individual characteristics was a unique experience. Each man knew innately this was his brother.

Chung, although Chinese was six feet tall, wore size eleven shoes, had twinkling green eyes that crinkled at the edges and seemed to see through you when he was doing business.

Six feet three inches tall, Farimo had the swarthy Egyptian look with stately nose, those same hazel crinkled eyes and was able to fathom your very soul.

Constantine was shortest of the four, he was a stout five feet, eleven inches. Built like a bear with curly dark hair covering most of his body. There were rumors about women who went mad for his hairy chest. He had flashing dark eyes and a disarming grin with the ability to turn frozen hearts into bubbling honey.

Garland was most like his father, six feet, five inches tall, a neon smile that flashed on/off, hazel eyes looking straight into the heart, clearing away the fluff, seeing only the real person, hiding there.

The brothers looked hard seeing something of themselves in each of the others and as always liking what they saw of their father's straight forward honesty in each person who faced them.

Each brother had spent no less than a year in the country and business of each of the others. They understood the ethnic backgrounds. Their father's idea of visiting a country by living as a native had been implemented in his sons. Constantine a known chameleon could go from Greek to Arabic to a South American country in a 24 hour period without changing his suit. Vernon had always insisted, "It's the small, the intimate, the personal characteristics that make nationalities unique. Otherwise, we'd all be alike."

When Garland was told he would spend a year in China, he could only think of Chinese as short, slant eyed people. His father told him, "Once you see flashing dark eyes clouded with tears because their special love hasn't shown, you will know one world and share the same emotions are shared."

Garland went. He learned how to be calm, to accept what he could not change and started understanding that all peoples have the human survival quest deep in each heart.

In Egypt Garland spent ten months with a family of shepherds following their flocks from one hillock to the next, ever alert for hazards. The young lambs were prey to roaming dogs or other predators. One sheep alone could freeze to death or run until it fell in its tracks looking for the flock. He spent almost a year studying Nile antiquities and the river itself, with all its life giving wealth and death. If the waters are badly managed, thousands starve when the waters recede due to a drought. The Nile's ephemeral beauty has given life and taken it away for millions of years, although the changes in its course have been few, he learned it remains the everlasting river of life.

Constantine took Garland along as part of the camera crew on a trip deep into the Amazon where they filmed the search and discovery of the Rio Poco head waters trickling its way from the Andes peaks to the gushing Amazon.

Vernon would not allow any of them to take over their businesses until they learned three eternal truths –

reverence for antiquity, the joy of discovery and brotherhood among men. As they sat with expectation of the coming problems each person had no qualms about trusting his brothers.

Chung started the discussion. The three other men each had infinite respect for their older brother and mentor. Chung had a sixth sense about economic stability of a situation. Chung's loyalty to their father had become legend in the family and literally had allowed the empire to be established.

From the time in 1945 when Vernon Velgrove walked into the Hong Kong sewing mill where Chung Kim Lee then twenty years old had worked for five years, first as a runner moving the fabric from bin to bin as the cutters needed it, then as a cutter, supervisor and later manager of his section. His quick mind assimilated millions of small details, analyzing and making split second decisions. In 1945 on December 16th Vernon Velgrove appeared at the door of Chung's small cubicle office and asked permission to enter. Chung felt immediately at ease in the presence of the big tall American with his western cut jacket. Chung stood there staring as Vernon clasped his hand and flashed the smile. Chung's heart was beating fast with the astonishment and recognition bursting upon him. Chung knew this was indeed that person his mother loved. On cold rainy nights huddled together to get the warmth from each other the mother told her small green eyed son stories about the tall American who had stayed with them and stolen her heart for all time.

Under the cherry tree in spring Ling Mei Su told her son, "Someday the mythical 'Velon' will come see you, Chung. When he left, he promised to return."

That handshake, the flash of the hazel eyes and the all encompassing disarming grin, told Chung that all the myths his mother told him were indeed true.

"You are Chung, Chung Kim Lee. You are Ling Mei Su's son?"

"Yes, Father." Chung said as he stared straight into those remarkable eyes.

Vernon Velgrove was momentarily taken aback. Years later, Vernon would reminisce saying, "When Chung said, Father, I was completely astounded that he would know. I had no idea his mother had told him of me. But even though I searched hoping to find my son I never dreamed Ling Mei would talk to him of her mixed up American Archeology student who suddenly left because his very old father was ill and probably dying."

He had only received one letter from her after he left saying she had given birth to a lovely son who had his father's green eyes and she was making her way to Hong Kong because bad times were coming and the British in Hong Kong would better understand her green eyed baby.

"I never heard another word. After the war I had to find her and do something to make things right, besides by then I wanted to know I had a son more than anything in the world. I used to ask myself over and over, "Why couldn't my wife in Texas have had that green eyed baby boy where I could care for him and raise him. Why does a man make a business if not for his heirs? And my heir is in China somewhere in a yellow river bed or in a Hong Kong ghetto or prison camp even. What would the Japanese captors do to a half-breed baby? So when Chung said, 'Hello, Father' it was the answer to all my prayers, dreams and solved all the problems of trying to explain how a tall American came to China and left a beautiful Chinese girl with child never to return. Those two words wiped away all the years of regret, all the doubt of whether or not to leave the boy alone. Why complicate an already mucked up situation? How do you explain to a twenty year old son that you are his never seen father? I had to know my son and if he was alive. Maybe I won't even tell the boy. I could help him anonymously. But I had to see my own flesh and blood. I wanted to know I had an heir, a son."

Vernon enveloped the shorter Chung in his arms and hugged him, pulled back, held his shoulders at arm's length and looked deep into his eyes. Both men had tears in their green eyes as Vernon Velgrove said, "Chung, I learned of your mother's death, if only I could have been here, maybe I could have done something."

"Oh, no, Sir. My mother would not have you blame yourself for not being with her. She always knew you would return. But I'm glad you have the love for her to care."

Vernon hugged his son again, still incredulous that they had such immediate understanding.

"Chung, I'm here to see if I can help my son get on in the world. When may we talk? I want to have a great deal to do with your future now that at last I've found you."

"Sir, I must finish my work here. May I see you this evening?"

"Come, when you finish. I'll be waiting for you. I'm at the Conrad Hong Kong Hotel on Queensway."

"I'll be there by six thirty."

"Good, until then, goodbye, my son."

"Goodbye, Father."

As Vernon Velgrove walked out into the Chinese sunshine he shook his head, turned, looked back into the clothing plant and smiled again, shook his head and walked to the waiting car.

The brothers were enjoying this rare occasion, remembering and talking of small things.

Suddenly Connie asked, "Do you still have Maybelline?"

Garland laughed, "Sure! But I've put her in an animal conservatory where she'll be cared for properly. I just couldn't do everything she needed in the end. She was too high maintenance."

Farimo asked, "Who is Maybelline?"

Garland replied, "She's a very lovable mountain lion, a cougar. She found me when I was eighteen and she was a few weeks old."

Connie added, "She grew up like a housecat."

"When Connie and I were living on our own at the ranch, if I ever brought a girl home, he would always open the bedroom door at the most inopportune time."

Connie broke up laughing, "You should have seen those girls run. When the cat jumped on the bed most girls jumped off running, but not Phyllis, she liked Maybelline. The cougar would run in the door jump in the bed's middle, snuggle in between Garlie and whomever and eventually start to snore."

The brothers all laughed at the cougar tales. Similar stories had been told before but it always made them feel more real to hear what their brothers did. Their Father had taught each of them to be unique and they had accomplished his wishes.

Farimo asked, "Chung, what happened when Kee Lei phoned about the car explosion on the bridge?"

Garland commented, "Yeah, I forget about that, did you phone it in to the police?"

Chung answered, "Sure we did. We've found almost any bomb causes the police to come to life in a big way. There are so many agencies involved in the harbor though, it's hard to know who to call."

Connie continued, "There's the LAPD, Sheriffs, LAFD, U.S. Army M.P., Navy M.P., U.S.C.G., Customs, Immigration, Border Patrol, Hazardous Materials, and one night I saw a car with U.S. National Police on it, and now Home Land Security trumps them all."

"Connie, do you still have headaches from the head bump you took in the Limo accident?"

"No, Garlie, not since I found Amanda, I don't think

about that anymore."

"Have you been back to visit the projection booth lately?" asked Farimo.

"Not since I found Amanda."

"Sounds like she solved lots of problems," Farimo laughed.

"You know it."

"I realize that's the reason you asked me to pick you up today," Farimo continued. "That wreck you had really screwed up VV for awhile, too. He thought everyone was out to get us. He always thought you would return though."

Connie said, "I never told you what happened, did I?"

Garland asked, "Come on let us hear the real story, Connie."

"Well the best I can piece together, this is the way it went. I was really tired from a trip up the Amazon and I had a shit load of film shipped back to the studio and the Limo was taking me there when it was hit from behind and in front at the same time. You know how they make those crazy stretch-outs well that one broke in two, right in the middle. I rolled out and lay in the gutter for awhile. The Limo was about a block away when it finally stopped. The police came and cleared the mess but they didn't see me."

"What'd you do?"

"When I rolled out I hit my head. I finally came awake and wandered down the nearest alley. I found a restaurant kitchen. The cook had just fired the dishwasher and asked if I needed a job. I couldn't remember. So I said yes and he put me to work right away. He gave me dinner. Later I found out it was a strip joint. I hung out there because the girls just thought I was homeless and one night the lighting guy was sick. I went up there and filled in for him and he never came back so that was my job."

"How did VV finally find you?" Farimo asked.

"I know that part of the story," Chung said.

"Yeah, Chung, how did you find me?"

"After several months the investigators came up with no trace of Connie. I was here for something else and VV was so distraught. I thought I would just go to the scene of the accident and see what I could find. I started asking around. I accidentally walked into the back alley and found the cook. He admitted they had a guy show up about three months before who didn't know his name."

Connie added, "When Chung came climbing up those steps to the lighting booth, I looked at him and knew he was my brother."

They all wiped their eyes and made scuffling noises. The whole family had looked for Connie, but Chung had gone to the right place.

Chung continued, "You should have seen the girls. They hung all over him. None of them wanted him to go. They had a party to celebrate his leaving. Do you ever see any of them?"

"Yeah, the cook works for me in Malibu and I've hired three of the girls for bit parts in movies. They saved my life, literally."

"The police were embarrassed after Chung found Connie just down the street, where they supposedly had searched and searched. It's like the police here in the harbor. They probably stumble over each other," Farimo added.

"Yeah, just like in the harbor. I know I would if there were that many people trying to do my job," Garland commented. "I wonder what VV would do about all those cops."

Farimo quickly responded, "He would investigate them and find out what they really do. He hated people who shirked their jobs and nosed into other's businesses. One time he was in Egypt with me and one of Mubarak's relatives came into the factory for truck parts. VV asked for a bill of lading approval by the payment department. Of course the guy had none of that and expected to just walk out with the parts and never be heard from again. When VV started making it real, the guy ran out of there and we never saw him again."

Chung, "Yes, VV knew just when to be tough. And now we must know also."

Remembering their father fondly and times he shared pieces of wisdom brought the brothers together as a family even though they saw each other only once a year if they were lucky. They each had different stories to tell of their father, Vernon Velgrove. He had died three weeks after turning ninety in 1980. Near the end, he rarely left his house. He had taught all his sons well. Given them *the best education they would accept* and trained each of them in the businesses they would ultimately own as CEO. He kept close watch on them, knew exactly how every business was faring. When they came on their semi-yearly visits, sometime during that visit he would always ask, "Have you found Maggie Cogburn, yet?"

All the sons knew about *lost love*. The older two sons thought they had no father until he found them. After finding Chung, Vernon discretely contacted Farimo's mother and asked permission to visit their son. The other two sons had been kept in closer contact with Vernon Velgrove, but he had been very busy and often sent them to schools where they would be educated well. He tried to learn their best abilities, promoted and honed the best assets, giving every opportunity to their dreams.

Each knew Vernon could have let them live without knowing him at all. Each son knew what the 'lost' part of their father's life meant. He was missing one of his children and the mother he loved. They knew he loved each of their mothers, but Maggie Cogburn had taught him a lesson he never forgot. Ego is only fleeting, love is forever.

Since it was Vernon's father's first business, Vernon kept separate the New York banking conglomerate called Velgrove International Industries Inc., NY. He had saved the New York Company hoping it would go to the heirs of Maggie Cogburn. He had the company running smoothly and the four 'boys' as he called them took turns running it by remote control. Until recently they each had spent several months a year in New York making sure the dealings were realistically reported. However, in the last couple of years, the oldest grandchild, Sun-Fo Lee, better known as Charlie, had taken over most responsibility at the New York Company. Everyone had been relieved and ready to let the company go since they were all busy with other projects. Charlie didn't get in the way much. He was young and had lots of partying to do.

Constantine had found information proving Maggie had a daughter, Eileen, but all knowledge after that was a mystery. He had never found any further information about Maggie or Eileen. It was as if they had been swallowed into an abyss.

Vernon was sorry he didn't marry Maggie. They were just kids in college, playing around. When she told him she was pregnant, he stammered and hesitated just that minute too long. Maggie was such a proud Irish girl. She turned on her heel, ran off and he never saw her again. A rumor at school said she had gone home to marry someone.

Vernon spent the next few years, first contrite, then remorsefully heartbroken. As WWI came along he knew Europe had nothing for him, so he spent the next few years wondering why he was so foolish to hesitate. Afterward, following his life's dream of finding antiquities, he traveled to China. There was a tremendous archeological dig going on in 1915 along the *Silk Trade Route*. He spent seven years there searching for unique, in situ, Chinese artisan tools and discoveries.

He found Mei in Canton. Mei's father was the local ombudsman negotiating Chinese workers for the dig.

Fearing a war was about to start and trap Vernon in that far off land Vernon's father, Henry, wrote his son demanding he return home to Texas immediately. The elder Velgrove told his son to come home because he was very ill and expected to die soon. He didn't just say he thought a war was beginning, but led his son to believe he would never see his father again alive. Vernon got on a plane and flew home where his father was recovering from an appendix operation and since Japan had invaded Hong Kong and northern China he could not return to China. It was years before Vernon could return to find Mei and his son.

As the boat rhythm became smoother out in deeper water, steadiness settled on the inside as well as the ocean. It was time they began discussions.

Chung started, "As you saw in the communiqué, we are being blackmailed. It is not as bad as it seems."

Constantine jumped in, "I think he's just a little punk, college kid trying to save the world."

"Aww, Connie," chimed in Garland, "you know who he is. He will do the right thing, if he has any DNA at all."

Connie laughed, "Yeah, that's what Farimo said."

Farimo Abba sat there looking like the black Buddha, shaking his head.

Chung said, "We each went through similar times in our lives. We just don't have Father here to tell us absolutely what is what."

"Ya'll know VV would have put him in charge of the New York office and made him earn his keep before he got to make demands." Garland said, always the Southerner.

"What a joke," Connie jibed, "Maybe he can be in charge of the T-squad and after the first attack we won't have to worry about him."

Farimo responded immediately, "We cannot put him in jeopardy, VV would turn over, you know. He spent so much time finding him; we must honor his wishes."

Connie says, "Ironic isn't it, now he finds us. What kind of degree of separation is that?"

"But you know as well as I, Father would not have caved in to this threat." Chung said ignoring Connie.

Garland, who always had a knack of seeing all sides, said, "Maybe putting him in New York is the answer. It will keep him plenty busy. We hire a Special Ops Team, train them and have them waiting and what's his name, Marko, makes the decisions when they are used. By then he'll be so involved with his Input-Output work he won't know what's happening."

"I think you just did it again," Connie said.

Farimo hesitated and said, "That could work out well."

Chung just nodded his head and thought about it.

Garland continued, "If he is tied up with decision making that's a good test to tell how much supervision we need in place."

Connie added, "Daddy, would have made him

demand to be in charge. That's the way he treated each of you. The only way you got to run your own businesses was by dragging it away from VV, and he kicking and screaming all the way."

They all laughed, remembering their own experiences with their father.

Farimo added, "VV always made you earn it."

They all knew the signal; Chung stood, cleared his throat and spoke. "So, we each take him into our businesses for a quarter. That gives us a year to become accustomed to his ways. During that year we hire a Special Ops Unit and start training. He can have input to their training…"

Connie blurts, "Let him train with them."

They all grinned. Connie's humor kept them in a light mood, but they all had seen his other side or as they called it *the Greek*.

Chung continued, "What I was going to suggest is he can determine when they are fully trained and when to use them. If in the mean time he can contribute to the NY office we will be ahead of the game."

They all moved nervously and made thinking noises. Farimo spoke first, "I can use some help with Input-Output. I would like to have him in Egypt first."

Garland assents, "Yeah! I could use sometime to get ready down in Houston. The Oklahoma office is moving and we're in deep shit right now. Maybe you could give me a turn in six months."

"I'll take him in three months. I'll introduce him to the world." Connie nods to his brothers.

"How old is this guy?" asked Garland.

"He's thirty-three years old," Chung answered. "He has a doctorate from Harvard in Economics, masters from Berkeley School of Business and three years at UCLA studying international law."

"Wowie! Sounds like he's tailor made for us." Connie said.

Chung continued, "He should be able to run NY office."

"Only if the DNA stuck," says Connie.

"Kids are coming out of school these days with less knowledge than a street pan-handler," Farimo stated.

Garland adds, "I say again, too bad VV's not here, he'd deal with it just like he did with us."

Chung adds, "We will fix all that. He just doesn't realize what he has gotten himself into. Let's talk to him and see how bright he really is."

As their attention returned to the present, elder son, Chang Kee Lee stood, raised his glass in toast, "Here's to Vernon Velgrove."

CHAPTER 8
MARKO WORRIES

Marko Fushier was so nervous waiting at the San Diego Yacht Club, he couldn't even drink. He sipped at his Perrier and pretended it was Scotch. He didn't know who this girl was sitting beside him, but she was sure cute. He wished Doug Henry were here. He would know how to handle these people and their harassments.

Logically, Marko knew Doug Henry could not be part of this escapade, he only had himself to blame for the outcome. When he caught his breath after reading that horrendous headline, the first call was to Doug's home in California. Then Marko called *the office*. After identifying himself, he was told to come with three forms of ID to be checked before they could give any information concerning Mr. Henry.

The office was a front for Henry and three other operatives when they were active. Since Henry had accidentally killed his hostage, he had not gone back to work. The *Office* always had a very pretty secretary named Mary Jo, Mary Louise, or Mary something. The handler who hired them must have a really hard time remembering names. Marko had met his wife, Maryellen at an Embassy party. Marko made an appointment with Fred Hoskins for the next day and flew to Washington, D.C. that night, stayed in a dumpy Traveler's Inn Hotel and saw Fred at 9:00am.

"Mr. Hoskins, if any person on this planet knows how to find my mother and father, Doug Henry does. He will find a way. I'm going where he is whether you help me or not."

"Well, Marko, that's pretty tough talk. I know Doug Henry also. He has not been the same since his incident. You may want to rethink your decision."

"Doug Henry could be crippled, half dead, wounded and unable to talk and he would point in the right direction, you've seen him work."

"Yes, I'm afraid I have. But he is not the same, I tell you that."

"Mr. Hoskins are you going to help me find him or should I leave?

"Okay, okay, here. All I can do is give you a map of approximately where he may be and suggest you get assistance in the village, Sacra."

"If you get me close, I'll do the rest. And I will be beholden to you and your agency."

As Hoskins showed Marko out the door with the promise of an airplane ride to the Bolivian Capitol he said, "Son, you don't want to say that about being beholden, you never know what might happen."

When Marko reached La Paz, Bolivia, an operative met him and explained, "Henry's in Bolivia about 300 miles from Ixiamas but he's in the Andes. I believe I've found someone who delivered supplies to him. You'll take the Andes express train going to Sacra."

CHAPTER 9
MARKO IN BOLIVIA

In Sacra Marko was met by Ophelia, a Spanish speaking woman who took him to the hotel. The next morning she knocked on the door to his room and said, "Senor, breakfast downstairs in thirty minutes. Take your things, we eat and leave."

They went three days by donkey to a village where she hired a guide to take Marko 'up the mountain'. As Ophelia left she said, "You are crazy, you know that, yes?"

"Thank you Ophelia, for everything. Here is one thousand dollars. Please take five hundred and keep five hundred to pay Carlos when he returns."

"That is too much, thank you. I will wait here for one week in this village, if you do not return by then I will leave and probably never see you again."

Carlos was his guide up the mountain. After four hours going straight up, passing through clouds and breathing shallow breaths quickly, they came to a plateau. There was a small lake and an abandoned mine for shelter.

The next morning Marko felt more adapted to his new climate, atmosphere or lack of oxygen. He could not imagine how hard this climb would be if he did not ride a bike in Boston. After hitch-hiking there he had used a bike as his only transportation for almost five years now, boiling humidity or freezing snow. As he rested he thought how surreal this was. He would never have predicted he would be sitting here in a cave in the Andes in some country; he wasn't sure whether it was Peru, Bolivia or Chile.

Marko Fushier, Berkeley School of Business graduate studied UCLA International Law three years before he started investigating "Tableau Economiques" written by one of his ancestors, Francois Queenay. It showed how income follows through the Economic System and when Wassily Leontief won the Nobel Prize in 1973 for his inter-industry analysis, sometimes called 'Input-Output' system, Marko quit UCLA Law School, hitch-hiked to Boston and during the next two years at Harvard took every class taught by the soft-spoken foreign accented lecturer until Leontief left Harvard in a huff moving to NYU.

While Marko was doing his doctoral thesis, *Political Decisions and World Economy Interaction* Leontief took a personal interest. Marko had Leontief's backing while finishing the document and degree. Now as Harvard Business School Doctor of Economics, he taught three classes and had an office at one of the most prestigious universities in the world.

That life was only one week ago. How fast life

changes. Sitting on the edge of the world, looking for his mother and father, what more was in his future? He knew now he must pay more attention to the people he loved. "Never forget to say, I love you. You may never have another chance."

Marko and Carlos finished their power bars and started walking. About noon Carlos started to act jittery.

Marko asked, "Do you need to stop?"

He said, "No."

Finally Marko demanded, "Carlos, what is wrong?"

"Well, you see, senor, this man, Mr. Henry, he is very strange."

"Really. How?"

"If he sees us first, he will shoot."

"Carlos, are we very close?"

"Senor, I think it is so. But I have only been here one other time and I left all the supplies up on that level ground above here."

"Carlos, are you afraid for your life?"

"Oh yes, yes senor. My family would not have food if I did not do this, so you see I must go on."

"Carlos, you go with me to the ledge. When you return, to Senora Ophelia she will give you money for me."

"Oh, senor, I could not ask for more."

"Carlos, you will not ask for more. You see Ophelia she will take care of things."

They made it to the ledge. Carlos stacked the supplies and took the two donkeys back down the hill. Marko took out his Harvard tee shirt put it on and started to walk up the hill towards some trees at the top.

As the trail opened wide the dogs started to bark, a donkey brayed and a rifle shot whizzed nearby. Marko held open his jacket showing the shirt.

After ten more steps, "I don't care if you did go to Harvard. Don't bother me."

"I have supplies for you, Doug Henry."

"I didn't order nothing, this is a scam."

"I have a chocolate torte from Mimi's in town."

"Who are you?"

"Why, Doug, you're slipping. This is Marko."

"Marko? Marko Fushier? Why boy, get on up here. Do you need some help carrying all that chocolate torte?"

"It couldn't hurt, Doug."

After that every thing went smoothly. Doug's helper, Romero, came down and carried supplies, pushed the mule Marko had ridden and finally got all the things up onto the porch.

Doug had taken a wife which surprised Marko. Doug said, "The Mapuches are the same Indians in Bolivia. They have women who really know how to live in the highlands. Aymaras, 'children of the sun' are different. They have kept their customs but integrated into the white culture. Nissa is a Mapuches. She followed me for months looking and digging until I couldn't live without her."

"She's beautiful in a way," Marko replied.

Doug grinned, "I never thought any woman would ever want to be with me forever. She really had to convince me."

"You should have known better."

"Well, she saved my life at least three times, maybe more."

"That's a real keeper, don't you think?" Marko stared off into the dark and thought about his Mother.

"I know you're thinking about your parents, I can see it." Doug continued, "If you get in the way, the Supremenistas will just eliminate the road block. We have to appear to be involved in another activity."

Marko noticed the 'we' but just continued, "I have some investments I could liquidate. We could hire some archeologists to locate areas for a probable dig."

"That's an excellent idea," Doug continued, "if you start soon, we can get up the mountain before the rainy season starts and we'll be above the deluge, but it'll be cold, really cold."

"Can you make the plans for me, Doug?"

"You knew I would. Of course I knew why you were here. The Mimi chocolate helped though."

After that Nissa brought in food. She served the meal then curled up beside Doug like a cat while they ate a long leisurely meal. Marko had never seen Doug so happy. This woman had changed his whole demeanor.

Later they sat on the porch, talked about old times of surfing in Malibu, digging in Montana, and finally about Marko's parents.

CHAPTER 10
MARKO GRIEVES

When Marko was sitting on top of a mountain in Bolivia grieving and reading the mail, at least he was safe. This girl beside him, the one the brothers sent to watch him, was probably a stone cold killer. "How did this all happen? Simple, I became an idiot."

"Marko, get a grip."

"I thought I could rule the world, I guess, like they do."

Marko was rambling, "First, I realized those two companies, one in China and one in Egypt, had manipulated the price of steel in China. By making cotton, soy beans, rice and Egyptian oil available to China they took the prices of steel and all automotive parts into the world of high finance. Then I found that company in Holland, was really owned by the brother in Texas. Afterward it was simple to figure out the rest."

Nancy replied, "I don't really know about all that. I'm just here to make sure nothing happens to you while they are discussing the situation."

"If you think they're going to kill me, would you please tell me?"

"Com'on, Marko, nobody of that group will hurt

you." She shook her head. "Don't be silly."

"Nancy? That is you're name isn't it?"

"My real name is Mei-Ling Lee, but Nancy is my Christian name."

"You're a Christian?" Marko paused, "I thought you'd be Buddhist or something."

"My father is Taoist, but my mother went to Catholic School and converted."

Nancy had been listening to Marko shake and quake for two hours. She felt sorry for him. He was trying to do something noble but had taken on the sons of Vernon Velgrove and didn't have any idea who he had attacked. She didn't know everything about the four brothers and their companies but she had seen many of the triumphs and a few of the failures. That Egyptian cotton conglomerate Farimo Abba ran was always right on the brink of disaster. She had seen her father spend many restless nights trying to solve meshing together these businesses without calling attention to their joint ventures.

Marko twisted on his bar stool and said, "How long do you think it will be?"

"Probably not too much longer." She said, trying to placate him.

"I can't just sit here and wait."

"They will call when they are coming into the harbor."

"Do you know I had over five thousand emails after we came out of the forest," Marko said as if so tired he couldn't quite think. "I call it the forest because I couldn't see the trees, Heh, heh."

"What'd you do then?" Nancy figured she should keep him talking.

"I read some and deleted the rest," Marko sighed.

"Weren't you afraid you'd lose something really important?" Nancy asked.

"I lost my mother and father, what's more important than that?"

"Oh! I see what you mean."

Marko began, "After Doug Henry decided to help me, it was inevitable we would eventually find mother and father. We had information gathered by the government agencies tracing the Supremenistas from Buenos Aires to Cordoba. They were going straight for the mountains. At Cordoba they split into several smaller groups. The first group took the Americanos; another group took the German Ambassador south along the Atlantic Coast to Bahia Blanco then to Viedma where the local police found his body in an abandoned house. After the papers and television broadcast warnings and threats, the third group took the Argentinean Ambassador to Corrientes where he was left at his family home."

"Doug said to me, "Look. The first group left Cordoba going directly to San Juan on the border. The Central Andes Mountains extends 5500 miles (8850 km) along the western coast of South America from northern Colombia to Cape Horn separates Argentina and Chile. The Andes are the longest mountain range, above sea level, and the second highest range in the world. The Supremenistas are not giving up and they maneuvered their group along the top of the Andes, crossing the border into Chile and then returning to Argentina until they reached San Salvador de Jujuy. Now they can go into the Saltan Seas. If they enter Bolivia, who knows where it will lead, this immense Andes system has numerous active volcanoes and a slow uplift continues building the Andes today. Snow covers the higher peaks of the range. Some peaks rise to over 20,000 feet (6100 meters) above sea level."

Doug always added history when describing old things. Following the trail he led them north. Marko and Doug rode the train running along the top of the Andes. During the travels Doug kept explaining how the mountains were formed and when in history. The interesting details kept Marko from being bored. They saw the blue waters of Paloma Reservoir, a recreational lake folding into Tontal Range and the Valle Fertil Range of western Argentina. Doug said, "The rocks of these ranges are ancient compared to the younger volcanic peaks and ranges of the Andes. The city of San Juan, Argentina on the eastern base of the Tontal Range is home of the Leoncito Astronomical Complex has the Jorge Sahade 2.15 meter telescope with a Ritchey-Chretien Reflector. The Leoncito Astronomical Complex is one of two observatories located within El Leoncito National Park. This area of the country rarely sees cloud cover. The other facility is the Carlos U. Cesco Astronomical Station of the Félix Aguilar Observatory. The observatory was established in 1983 by an agreement between several universities and the Argentine government. Operation began in 1987 and the complex is now the Argentine national facility for ground-based astronomical observations. The Supremenistas originally planned to take over one of the observatories near San Juan. When the escaping party arrived at the Felix Aguilar Observatory, they were surprised to see armed men walking the perimeter. So the Guerillas decided to move further into the mountains. They were riding in a Ford Explorer followed by a Toyota Landcruiser. They took a train at Villazon, border with Bolivia. Luckily they arrived on the day the train was running."

When I asked, "How far behind them are we?"

Doug answered, "I'd say a week at least, maybe two. They've been lost to the tracers since they arrived in Uyuni a town on the edge of two salt flats, the world's largest, Salar de Uyuni or Salar de Tunupa is 10,582 square kilometers (4,086 sq mi). Located near the crest of the Andes in southwest Bolivia, at 3,656 meters (11,995 ft) elevation above sea level, the Salar resulted from transformations of several prehistoric lakes. It's covered by a few meters of salt. The crust serves as a source of salt and covers a brine pool, exceptionally rich in lithium. It contains 50 to 70% of the world's lithium reserves, which is in the process of being extracted. The large area, clear skies and exceptional surface flatness make the Salar ideal for calibrating the altimeters of the Earth observation satellites. The Salar serves as the major transport route across the Bolivian

Altiplano and just so you know, it's a major breeding ground for several species of pink flamingos."

I asked Doug, "What is the Altiplano?"

He kept on talking about the area we were going past. Doug can't help himself so I just listened to his information. "Salar de Uyuni is part of the Altiplano of Bolivia. A high plateau formed during uplift of the Andes. The plateau includes fresh and saltwater lakes as well as salt flats and is surrounded by mountains with no drainage outlets. Salar de Uyuni spreads over 10,582 square kilometers (4,086 sq mi). Have you ever been to the Bonneville Flats in the US?"

I said, "I saw it when I was hitchhiking to Boston."

"Well Salar de Uyuni is roughly 25 times the size of Bonneville Salt Flats in the United States." Doug continued, "The center of the Salar contains a few "islands", which are remains of ancient volcano tops which were submerged during the era of Lake Minchin. They include unusual fragile coral-like structures and deposits consisting of fossils and algae."

"We were going through the Andes forever I just stared out the window awhile and Doug nodded off until we felt the train slow and stop. We were on a second rail, waiting for another train to pass going south. Doug stood up and said, "Let's get some food. We still have hours to go."

I said, "Sure."

As we walked down the corridor there was a rumbling then the other train passed. We went to the dining car. It consisted of vendors selling food they had prepared some where else. We bought sodas and some really strong coffee and rolls. Doug said, "I'm not very adventurous with the local food, but if you want to try it go ahead."

"I'll just follow your lead. It looks good and eventually, I'm sure we will need to eat more substantially."

The train started again and we returned to our seats to find someone setting there. An old woman with bags of clothing was piled into the seats. The other people standing in the aisles with bags and bundles looked at us to see if we would complain. When Doug walked past her and went to the observation platform there seemed to be a sigh of relief from the packed train car. After standing for awhile, we looked up to the train roof as it curved around a bend. Atop the train were people lying on blankets. Doug asked, "Do you have a camera? Maybe you should take this spectacular landscape. If you bought a blanket from that old woman, you could probably get a good deal."

I went back inside the train car, made the purchase and came back with the woolliest, thickest blanket I had ever seen.

As I walked back I saw Doug swing off the side onto a ladder going up the train's side. We found a spot and wedged between some support beams. It felt secure, the air was fresh and I began to take pictures.

Doug warned me, "Be aware, there are some tunnels along the way, just don't let it catch you standing."

I asked, "How did you end up down here?"

Doug Henry answered, "Funny, I was thinking about that when you came up that hill the other day. I was sitting on the front porch watching the setting sun reminiscing."

"I ended up here because I read an account about Hiram Bingham's 1911 discovery of Machu Picchu – Inca citadel "Temple of the Moon" located 9,000 feet above sea level in Southwest Peruvian Andes."

Doug visited that archeological dream. There wasn't really an excavation. It was so high in the Andes the discovery only had to be recognized and logged and verified by age.

As fascinating as the discovery was Doug looked for his own mystery to solve. He spent two months renting every dilapidated aircraft available. He mapped and aerial photographed the miles and miles of mountains, forests – every possible terrain trying to find a possible lost city. Macchu Picchu must have sister cities. Then one day he was staring at his photos from across the mountain in Chili, when he compared the photo taken in October as the thaws were beginning with Dec or the beginning of summer. He found what he hoped for – some crumbled walls and a mound on the hillside overlooking a verdant river valley.

Doug decided the easiest way to keep strangers out was to buy the mountain side. The land was cheap. He was thought to be a rich eccentric, aren't all Americans crazy. The crazy American even built a hacienda. Hired a family to come and keep the house and grounds and help with the intended work.

Three weeks ago Doug Henry had been sitting there staring into the January sunset. These were the longest days of the year with sunrise at 5:00a.m., setting between 8:30 to 9:00 pm. Doug found an Incan Statue that day. Sitting on the stoop exhilarated with his luck and bone tired from the dirt moving work and strain of the painstaking tedium when he realized they had opened a burial cache for some elevated soul.

In the last glimmering of sunlight Doug saw the splash of metal in the ravine. Coming up the hill were five donkeys and two men.

He immediately went inside and told his wife, Nissa, "We have company coming, could you put water on to boil? The travelers will be hungry and want to wash."

By the time the climbers reached the hill top aerie of the former Treasury Agent, the water was boiling, the stew was ready and there was a chill in the air as the night breezed through the pines.

Bark, the English bulldog, watched as the four curs did their announcements and made sure the small party knew they had walked onto private property. Doug fired his shot to alert the intruders. Marko came up the hill and started talking to Doug.

Soon we were on our way to find mother and father. The train ride continued seemingly forever.

Doug asked, "Do you want to hear about the terrain here?"

I said, "Sure thing. Since we have time to talk, you could tell me what you're looking for in your digs."

"I love to talk about that stuff. There's no problems, no one trying to kill me and I can go anyplace I please to investigate. The record of siliceous sponges-Hexactinellida and demosponge "Lithistida" hinges on both body fossils plus isolated spicules mostly recovered from limestone by acid digestion. The earliest record of siliceous sponge spicules was in the late Neoproterozoic of Hubei, southern China and Mongolia and body fossils attributed to the hexactinellids have been described from the Ediacaran of South Australia. They are the oldest-known representatives of extinct animal phyla. The Early Cambrian saw a remarkable diversification in spicules. Due to the Andean geology resulting from the eastward subduction of the Nazca tectonic plate underneath South America, the Puna is underlain by a steeply dipping plate sector. The Sierras Pampeanas zone however, is underlain by a sector of almost horizontal Nazca plate, possibly due to the subduction of the Juan Fernandez Ridge submarine mountain range. Ridges are topographic highs difficult to stuff down subduction zones, with profound effects on volcanism and upper plate structures. All that just shows how the Andes formed. But the real reason I'm digging here is Anthaspidellid sponges. Reportedly they range from the La Laja Formation in the Chica de

Zonda Range in the Precordillera Oriental, Argentina. Between Abra Pampa and San Pedro de Atacama is a range filled with the fragments of crabs and more or less well-defined dendroclone spicules. They are the only Cambrian occurrence of anthaspidellids known in South America. In 1920 Walcott reported from the Estancia San Martin Formation, of latest Early Cambrian and early Middle Cambrian age from San Isidro Gulch near Mendoza. Similar spicule assemblages occur in the La Laja Formation from the Chica de Zonda Range, in the Precordillera Oriental near San Juan, and that is where I have concentrated my excavations. In 1994 a protected area was created. With its peculiar vegetation, Puna and high Andean habitats together with the threatened species found there are historic sites, paleontological remains, and archaeological sites including a stretch of the Inca Trail. It is south west of San Juan province on the western Tontal range slopes. The nearest town is Barreal 34 km away. Uspallata, in Mendoza province, is 93 km distant. My fondest dream is to be able to work there."

I was amazed at the knowledge Doug had compiled in his brain and commented, "You must do it. You are so adamant nothing should stop you."

Doug continued, "After we arrive in San Salvador de Jujuy, I know every inch of the Cordillera Oriental territorial lay-out. That's where we will find your mother and father. There are tribes there who know me. They will be honest with me and tell me if there are outsiders nearby."

I said, "I hope this will be quickly. I know father needs medicine soon. My mother would have enough for a month at least but longer than that would be stretching reality."

As the train rumbled on up and down through tunnels and in long curving hillsides we stayed on top. The terrain was too bleak to encourage humans to live there. Rocks and gullies hundreds of yards deep made the landscape stark. After many stops and waits the train finally arrived at Salvador de Jujuy where Doug rented an old station wagon, put all our equipment in the back and started driving on Camino International No. 9. The road went through Volcan Caldo, Condor Pass, on to Pueblo Viejo where we spent time searching and asking questions. We retraced and went back across the Azull Pampa to Abra Pampa, a lush green area on the river running across the top of the Andes. We searched and found traces of the group but after reaching the border towns of La Quiaca, Argentina and Villazon, Bolivia. There was no hint of the Supremenistas having been there. It was as if they were swallowed into thin air. After waiting weeks for information, We were driving the beat-up old Chevy on Ruta Nacional 28 at the bend of the river coming from the mountain gorges a man standing on the roadside waved us down. He said, "You are senior Doug?"

Doug answered, "Yes, and you are Alberto, right?"

"Oh yes, sir. You remembered me."

"Do you need a ride, Alberto?"

"Oh no. I was sent to take you to Viejo Carl. He would speak to you."

Alberto got into the car and we drove several miles into the bush, then walked for another mile to cabins in a secluded valley where we were treated to a meal and drinks and afterward the chief or Viejo Carl as he preferred, told us a story of the outsiders who brought two Americans to their camp and left them there three weeks ago with the missionary woman. The missionary woman was a medicine woman and tried to help them but they were extremely ill with the fever and died. I didn't understand all the talk, but we knew this was the end of our journey.

Doug said, "Viejo Carl, this is their son. We have been searching for them and he is grieving for his parents."

Viejo Carl rose and said, "Then he must grieve no more. They are at peace here. I have honored them with burial in our best places overlooking the waterfall. They were good people who showed love. That is difficult for outsiders sometime. They were people of the sun as we are. Come, I will show you where they rest."

Doug knew I didn't understand what they were saying completely, but I understood enough to know they were dead and I was already standing with tears streaming down my cheeks.

Doug said, "These people are the Aymaras, people of the sun. They have honored your father and mother by burying them in their favorite grave yard."

I sat all night between the graves talking to my parents. I told them of my love, how I had searched, how I would avenge their death someway and how dreary my life would be without them. By morning I was drained and Doug said we must go. I walked into the lush forest beside the waterfall and found hundreds of orchids growing wild there. I carefully took two plants and arranged them on the graves. I said goodbye and left. Doug drove back to Villazon arriving at the Estacion Central just before the arrival of the weekly train. We slept for two days on the train to Sucre, Bolivia where we hired the river boat going upstream and borrowed donkeys to go up the mountain to Doug's home.

Marko was still reliving his trip through the Andes when he realized he was terribly hungry and turned to Nancy who had been listening to his story, "Couldn't we just go somewhere and eat?" Marko pleaded.

Nancy answered, "They said I should keep you here. It's safer and they will know where we are. If you want to eat, the dining room here is excellent. Com'on, let's go check it out."

Marko rose, "Alright, I don't know if I can eat anything or not."

The two young people walked into the dining room. Out the window they saw the one hundred foot REGAL SONJIA swing around and back up to the dock making a Mediterranean landing in front of the yacht club.

Marko said, "Oh dear, now it begins."

Nancy took his hand and patted it saying, "It'll be

alright. Do you have any idea who you're dealing with, Marko?"

"Yeah, I know."

"Com'on let's go out and help them dock the boat."

CHAPTER 11
MARKO INTERROGATION

Marko liked Nancy, she was Oriental cute. She liked him too he could tell. The two of them walked out of San Diego Yacht Club onto the dock where the REGAL SONJIA laid out a gangplank from the boat's rear step. Nancy was holding Marko's hand as she guided him up the ramp.

Nancy took him into the stateroom below and introduced him to the oldest brother. "This is Chung Kee Lee, may I freshen up, father?"

"Very glad to finally meet you, Mr. Fushier, this is Farimo Abba."

Did Nancy say 'father'? Marko shook hands and wondered what was happening.

"How do you do, I have heard of your excellent education in economics. Father sent me to Harvard also, but then there was no Input-Output department."

As Marko answered he noticed the boat was moving, "There is no Input-Output department now. After Dr. Leontief moved on to New York, it was called Macroeconomics."

Marko was confused by what was happening. They

said come aboard and almost immediately the boat started moving. They were leaving the harbor. He didn't know where they were going. If the boat was moving fast, by midnight they could be half way to Mexico. He decided he must settle down and deal with these guys. After all, he had requested a meeting. These were the richest and most powerful men in the world and he was challenging them, their business dealings and demanding they fight terrorism. But here they were asking him questions and listening as if his answers were important to them. He had expected them to be belligerent towards him, not like this. The only good part was these men were taking him seriously. That was really astonishing. Originally he thought maybe they would try to threaten him or even kill him. He had spent so many restless nights tossing and turning trying to figure out the best way to approach them. Now they were treating him like a person of knowledge and shaking his hands. There must be something going on he did not understand. I guess they could still do that, kill me. How he let them get him on this boat was still a mystery.

That Nancy was so calm and nice and then the next thing he knew they were going out to sea. Here's Nancy now. "Nancy, where'd you go?"

"Oh, don't worry. I can't get off the boat now. We are heading out to have a lovely sunset dinner in Catalina."

Farimo Abba took his hand and guided him over to the short curly haired guy. "This is Constantine

Koulas, the movie maker. You may have seen *The Dust over Israel.*"

Connie shook Marko's hand, guided him over to Garland, while saying, "Marko Fushier, that name sounds very familiar, could you be related to the Argentine Ambassador?"

"That is my uncle, Pierre. He took my father's place after the terrorists took them...my father and my mother."

"Terrible, terrible incident." As Connie guided him to a chair beside Garland, "Garland Velgrove, this is Marko Fushier. He won't need as much introduction as I supposed. His uncle is the Ambassador to Argentina. Marko you must know many people in the social circles I inhabit."

The tall Texan grabbed Marko's hand pumped it and continued to hold it. "Marko welcome to our world. Connie is the socializer for the world. He will turn up in Istanbul next week. Nobody knows where he'll be after that."

They all drew up chairs in a circle and Chung asked, "Now Marko Fushier, please tell us how you want to change the economic, social and materialistic traits of the world."

Marko looked at them all as they sat ready for his answer. He took a deep breath and started answering their questions. "Most of the world's problems are socio-economic. We could have avoided many wars with the power your companies possess. You, Chung Kee Lee, manipulated your Szechwan Province production of rice into spreading industrial jobs for thousands, making them happier and richer so they no longer wanted to revolt against the regime and the regime was pleased with the amount of extra taxes available for social programs."

"Farimo Abba, your company in Egypt has been dealing with the results of fiscal policies, International Monetary Fund arrangements during the 1990's, massive external debt relief due to the Gulf War coalition, privatization and new business legislation moving Egypt towards a market-oriented economy prompting increased foreign investment. The benefits failed to trickle down to the population experiencing underemployment and delivered living standards so low a youth protest demanded more political freedoms and forced President Mubarak to step down. You, however, managed to trade crude oil and petroleum products with your brother in China and turn cotton, textiles, and agricultural chemicals into relaxed price controls, reduced inflation, cut taxes and partially liberalized trade and investments. Agriculture has mainly been deregulated mostly due to your mother's family influence."

"Garland, your oil and gas companies are worldwide. The South American agricultural production, Netherlands banking, Swiss financial and venture banks and worldwide construction company all conquer many problems in various locations."

"Connie, I really don't know all your involvement except it fits through the New York Velgrove company and your International Films Distribution."

All the brothers looked at each other, smiling. Marko continued, "How did I do on first exploration into your very complicated interactions?"

Chung answered, "Not too bad, for an amateur."

Chung Kee Lee's next question, "Tell me Marko Fushier, how did you figure out we were, I believe you called it, manipulating the world economy?"

"How detailed do you want me to be?"

"Give us as much information as you can."

So Marko continued, "After searching for my mother and father in Peru and Bolivia, I was resting for awhile at Doug Henry's place in Chile so I asked my office assistant to send the mail I received during the six months I was gone. They sent my computer programs and all the letters, magazines and books. To catch up on the world happenings I started reading magazines in no specific order. I was reading the article in *Newsweek* about the Brazilian development by your Holland Company and the Chinese arbitration in the Philippines de-forestation project in the *Economist*. Then I read a local paper stating Bolivia was changing their rules on de-forestation. The new Forestry Law transferred power to municipalities and prefectures. New regulations changed the agrarian law merging the rights over the land and forest and since its approval, social, economic and ecological considerations constitute legitimate ways to justify land ownership. Previously, logger groups had no formal access to forest resources and were forced to operate illegally within areas granted as forest concessions. Having read in the *Economist* how Velgrove Enterprises owned about half the land in Bolivia. I started tracing the land purchases of all Velgrove Industries and that led me to the countries where you are involved."

"Eventually, I started an Input-Output spread sheet for each of your locations. It gave me information to make larger versions and eventually analysis of three Velgrove corporations. Chung Enterprises helped the Kutai Barat district in Indonesia develop a new district timber regime making it legal to transport timber out of the district. The lack of personnel and supporting infrastructure limited the government's ability to carry out efficient monitoring and enforcement. Under decentralization, the issue of conservation and protected areas must also ultimately be placed in the context of opportunities for local revenue-generation. In manipulating these various governments into decentralization of the forest usage has proven extremely lucrative for your companies."

Garland interrupted, "How does this transfer to terrorism?"

Marko took a deep breath and continued, "Your companies have a good handle on all the information of these countries and how they are governed. It would seem to me that you already know where the terrorists are located and track them systematically. You have your security squads for your various locations. It would be easy enough to train and use an expert group composed of ex-navy seals, army rangers, marines and other previously committed soldiers who were available and ready to solve the terrorist problems of the world. I don't want to minimize the dangers, but surely you have already considered something of this nature. Someone needs to carry through on this. The world can't just keep on being blown-up by idiots."

Connie jumped up and said, "Kid, you can't just go into a country and kill people."

"If you cleared the set-up with the United Nations beforehand, I think we can make it an approved group, possibly secretive, but sanctioned by most nations."

Whispering in the back of the room caught Marko's attention. "What are you discussing, Mr. Abba?"

"I was just bringing something to Garland's attention."

"Is it something we should all know?"

Connie jumped in, "You're a college professor, and I'll bet you keep those kids in line, don't you."

"Okay, I get the point. I do demand attention when I lecture, sorry for the academics."

They all laughed breaking the ice, before Marko went on talking about all the information he unearthed about the companies and the owners.

Garland commented, "VV, that's what we called our dad, Vernon Velgrove, would have been proud of you. Now what is this terrorist stuff you want?"

"You must form a crack soldier group who go into areas where terrorists are forming and take them out. Give these troops the training, equipment and communications to control terrorists. They're already basically trained. You have to train for the quick and dirty. I'm sure you have the power to arrange this. In the countries where you deal, you also have enough power and information to influence the governments."

With that start Marko went into details of how to research the terrorists groups, how to determine their ability to harm the world, and the economic distribution. The details went on for hours. The brothers listened to every word. He couldn't quite comprehend why they were so very interested in his ideas. But, he had an audience and he kept on going until he was so tired he could hardly hold up his head.

CHAPTER 12
DECISIONS ARE MADE

For hours he had been in the stateroom with all four brothers asking questions. They each seemed to have a definite area of expertise, but would change and each start on another subject. Marko was exhausted almost as much as when he was looking for his mother and father in the Andes.

Finally, they sent him below, because he was completely exhausted and couldn't even talk. Now he couldn't sleep. He just kept going over and over what they had asked him, trying to figure why they had asked the questions.

He had barely slept in seventy-two hours. As he sat up, there was a slight knock at the door. He opened it and was surprised, but not really. There stood Mei-Ling.

"May I come in?"

"Sure." Marko replied, "I can't sleep anyway."

"They asked me to leave the room. Only the brothers are in there now."

"Are they plotting to dispose of me?"

She grabbed him in a hug and said, "They don't do that, they're good guys."

She kept her arm around him as he sat down on the bunk. It just seemed natural that they lay on the bunk, fully clothed and she comforted him.

"I can tell you are a good person, Marko. I don't know why, but I have a good feeling about you."

"Yeah, I kind'a like you too. Maybe if we were in different circumstances we could follow through on those feelings."

"May I just lie here next to you until they call us for dinner?"

"I don't know about you, but this has been a very long day for me."

"Marko, where did you come from today?"

"Well, I came from New York on the midnight flight into Orange County Airport. And you? Where did you come from?"

"I only drove down from UCLA. I'm a grad student there. I'll have my doctorate by the end of this year."

"Wow, beautiful and educated."

"You silly."

"Yeah, I know. I have to lighten up a little. This whole thing is just so serious. I've never done anything this important before. I had help preparing for my doctorate even. But this time I just plunged in on my own. My pal, Doug Henry that I stayed with in Chile didn't even know what I was doing with all the information. I didn't want to involve anyone in case it got dangerous. I could take the chance, because of my mother and father, but I would never ask anyone else to put their life on the line just for me."

"Marko, you will soon find the brothers are not dangerous people. They are the kindest, most reasonable people you will ever meet. They are my family, too."

"I'm sorry, but I have grieved so much in the last year there is nothing left of me."

"It's okay, just try to relax. Let me rub your neck and back. You know how good we oriental chicks are at massage."

"You're funny, too."

As Mei-Ling rubbed the tight muscles in Marko's neck, he finally relaxed some and she giggled and talked about her school. She asked him questions about getting her doctorate and talked about familiar things. They finally lay side by side napping when a knock on the door startled them both.

"Please join the brothers in the stateroom," came from outside the door.

They jumped up and tried to straighten their clothes and hair. Marko answered, "I'll be there in five minutes, please."

"Thank you, sir."

They heard the sailor move down the hallway and knock. Mei-Ling knew he was knocking on her door. They waited for him to leave then she ran out and up the steps to the deck. As her uncle came from the bow of the boat she managed to arise from the stern deck.

"Miss Mei-Ling, please come to the stateroom. It's very important."

"Thank you, Uncle Luk."

CHAPTER 13
PLANNING FOR MARKO

While Marko and Mei-Ling were alone in his stateroom, the brothers were above deck talking of the future. When he finished demonstrating his knowledge, and was sent below to rest, the brothers deliberated the practical steps setting in motion plans facilitating Marko's training in the company's businesses.

As Marko left the stateroom and the door closed, Connie looked at each of them and said, "How about that DNA?"

Garland, Farimo and Chung laughed together. The atmosphere was definitely lighter than previously.

Chung, "The boy's fine."

Farimo, "He'll be an asset."

Garland, "I can sure use some of that knowledge of his for the Amazon project. Farimo, if you finish quickly, please send him on to me sooner than three months."

Farimo was thinking about their father, "What a joy it would be to see VV's face. He spent forty years trying to find this kid's mother and now he'll never know. On the other hand, maybe Maggie Cogburn, her daughter and the 'old man' are all sitting up there somewhere laughing at us for taking this all so seriously."

"You guys forget I have to introduce him around." broke in Connie.

Chung, "I'll work with him in Hong Kong starting January next year, by then he'll be ready, if we don't scare him to death sooner. We should tell him what we have planned so he can stop worrying about his welfare. Mei-Ling said he asked her to tell him if we were going to kill him."

Garland, "I think we should discuss bringing our relationships out into the open anyway."

Connie, "Yeah, if he can figure it out, so can other people. Cyber security is the most complicated security crisis we have. Nobody, from Sony to Lockheed, knows how to deal with it. Most try working behind the scenes with customers reacting to a breach after they're hacked."

"You're doing some of that, I'm sure, with your security company. Why don't we come out front? We'll take steps to make our companies Cyber safe and if somebody questions our connections, cyber security will be the reason for our conglomerate activities," Garland responded.

"Sure. It seems every breach has new information. Every company must learn its lessons from scratch and the public doesn't know what to expect," Connie replied.

Farimo, "I have already had approaches from Addi Ababa, my mother's cousin. He is a computer geek and had it mostly figured out we were helping each other. I think Cyber security is another product for sales to work on for all the companies."

Chung, "Then we must take it seriously. It will make our work a little more intense, but in the long run probably save us some negotiations. Your suggestions are well taken. We've needed to make this move for awhile."

Garland, "Good, I don't like being underhanded."

Connie, "Awe, com'on Garlie, you're not a kid any more, dad's not gonna kick your ass."

Garland, "I sure wish he were here to see his grandson perform like a true Velgrove."

Farimo, "He trained us all to appreciate that kid just like he would have. Now come on, we'll make him earn his keep."

Chung, "Here is my plan. First we send him to Egypt with Farimo. Let him use his education to help there. While he's busy learning the Egyptian circumstances, we will find an army to put in his hands when he returns. Connie, you already have a handle on this with your special security group. You get it going either as a part of your group or as a by-product. Garland, you will work with him in Texas and introduce him to the big company. Show him everything including your problem in Brazil and Oklahoma. He's been traveling in South America for a year; he should be well versed in the problems there. By then we will have figured out how to introduce our companies as Velgrove Industries. We may need to have the Velgrove

Industries NY buy some of the smaller companies, to cover negotiations previously made. He can come help me in China in the third quarter. Connie, by that time we will have the companies straightened out and you will be able to introduce him as the new CEO of Velgrove Industries, NY."

Connie, "What about Charlie?"

Farimo, "Chung, you are ignoring that problem. You don't want to admit Charlie's a problem. You know he won't go down easily. What are you going to do?"

"You're right Farimo. You always pegged me. Even VV knew that. What do you think I should do?"

Farimo, "Chung, you're eighty-six years old. Start giving him some of the Chinese companies. He and you will know very soon if he can do it. He won't have all his cronies to take the blame and he will have to buckle down and become a business man."

Chung, "If only he were as knowledgeable and aggressive as Mei-Ling. I can trust her with anything. I will deal with him quickly."

Garland, "That's a little different than I thought he needed. Charlie could have some training in oil and gas production. I could use him in Bolivia. We're in production down there. If he goes out and runs a rig, he'll come back a different guy."

Connie, "Charlie's not going to do that."

Garland, "How do you know? I think he will surprise us one day."

"Thank you. I appreciate your offers and concern. I must control my son. He will not be a further problem," commented Chung. "Now we must solve the Marko problem."

Garland, "I agree with the plans you laid out, Chung. Let's start with that. You know it changes as we move on with it."

Farimo, "It could work. Of course, it doesn't change anything for me much, just being stuck out there in the open without a leg to stand on. What do you think, Connie?"

"I see the reasoning doing it this way. I had hoped to get to him sooner, but I see how putting it off could make the introductions better. We'll have time to set up the security group and expand on that. Are we going to tell him he's family, or hold off?"

Garland, "I say we hold off."

Chung, "It would be very difficult not to tell him. He's going to wonder why we gave in so easily, if we do not tell."

"So, that's it, we tell him." Connie said, "He thought he couldn't talk before, wait until he hears this."

Chung, "I'll have them bring him back up from below. It should tell us a lot reading his reaction."

Connie, "Can't we just go to dinner now?"

Farimo, "Maybe that's a good idea. We can think about what to say."

Garland, "Okay, I give. If we tell him before, we can celebrate a new family member."

Chung, "I really think we need to tell him now, so he can stop thinking we're about to kill him."

Connie, "I guess you're right."

Farimo, "Okay, I'll make it unanimous."

CHAPTER 14
WHAT'S NEXT?

Chung hesitated a moment, "Let's investigate this terrorism situation between us before we involve Marko."

Connie proposed, "You all know I have the Horizon Industries already. Its running very smoothly right now, I'd rather not upset the balance we've attained. I know it would seem sensible to just expand that business and make it fit his demand, but I've thought it out and it seems to me we should create a new company so it's not traceable from any of our other companies."

"Connie, I agree entirely. Let's look at some options," Chung replied.

"Most of the terrorists have transitioned to the Mediterranean countries. In Egypt, we have plenty of desert training space," Farimo added.

Garland added, "You need more than just desert, I happen to know that in South Sudan there are mountains, swamps and all matter of climates. Maybe it would be better to train someplace like that."

"China has all matter of climates as you say and we could cover up the training there maybe by substituting a little tai-chi and judo," Chung laughingly suggested.

"Chung, we have to be serious with this," Farimo said.

Connie jumped up and shouted, "Come on you guys. We have to get down to business here. Terrorism is not a game. Besides, I'm hungry."

"We could probably do it in Texas on the ranch and not get too much attention," Garland said. "I understand Leslie Snipes set up a training situation in Tennessee, but the nosey neighbors complained."

"Come on guys! This is serious! We need expert help. It won't work without it. You must hire a green beret, navy seal or something to set this up properly," Connie declared.

Chung took charge as usual, "What if we hired a specialist and set training in Brazil. There is space there to train in different climates. If they train in the high altitudes where Bolivia and Peru meet, the soldiers will have more stamina. We could have more control of the area and facilities placement, don't you think, Garland?"

"Chung, you've hit it on the head again. The property there is more than adequate for setting up a training headquarters," Garland answered.

"If we put the company under the Brazil or even Bolivian laws it will be easy to cover the real purpose," Chung continued. "Garland you handle the set up. I will hire the training crew. Farimo you establish a group to follow the terrorists activities. Connie your best help will come in supplying information as you and your Horizon Group travel about the world."

Farimo added, "That sounds like a good plan, but what happens when we try to use the 'crack' group?"

Connie, "I believe we get validated by the United Nations or UNESCO or UNEP or some other governmental agency. Most people want something done about terrorism, its just nobody's figured out what steps to take. When I started to set up the Horizon Industries I had a lot of help from my friend who had been an Army Ranger for 30 years. He knew who to hire and how to train them."

"That's great, but how do we find someone like that, if we don't have a friend?" Farimo asked.

"Hold on, I'll call Moody and see if he has an idea about who to hire." Connie walked to the deck and dialed his cell phone. "Hello Moody, we have a situation here and I wonder if you can give me a little information. We need a body to run the solution I mentioned before I left on Friday. Do you have any ideas for an in charge person?"

"I understand what you are asking, I believe. Do you want a particular sex or could it be either?"

"Either, of course."

Moody kept asking questions, "Do you need this body immediately or in a few months?"

"Now would be better, I guess thirty days wouldn't be so bad."

"All right, I have two people in mind, male and female, I would have to find them and see when they're available."

"Let's go with them both. See when they can be at

the ranch. Okay?" Connie turned the cell phone off and went back inside. "Well I believe we may have someone to run the operation. Moody has both a man and a woman who will be at the ranch in thirty days or less to start."

"Hey, Bro! How about you come over to Cairo and help me for a day or two. You'd probably solve all my problems in a day and a half. You really move it, don't you," Farimo commented.

Chung said, "This is all well and good, but we need to lay down some ground rules, then negotiate with these people and set up the operation."

"Come on Chung, they will do it. They will do it right. We can get on with our work." Connie replied.

"How did you hire them so soon? You were only on the phone a few minutes."

"I have to cut through the muck, that's all," Connie responded.

Garland chimed in, "He's been that way all his life. You never wait for Connie."

Connie's phone rang. He took it to the deck again. "Hello Moody, what's up?"

Moody replied, "I got'em. Got'em both. They will be there in six days; they need to clean up something so expect them Monday morning."

"Great! Thanks for this Moody. I'll see you down below."

No one understood Connie's coded speech when he started talking in signs as Garland called it. They knew he was the best. He had just proven it. He had contacts in every field of expertise and used them frequently. People were only too happy to cooperate with Connie. He had the touch.

Chung stood and cleared his throat, "Well that is a good start on the project. Let's recap – in six days two experts will be at the ranch in Texas to plan and assemble a crew. After picking the members of the group, they will be transferred to Bolivia where Garland has a location picked. In three months the group should be prepared for testing and ready to go thereafter. Farimo, you will keep track of the terrorists in your area, I will track any abnormalities in my area and both Garland and Connie will be alert and find information during their travels which they'll pass on to Farimo's information group in Qatar. We can get an assist from the Rand Corporation statistical group already located there and segue off to our own Terrorist Statistics Group (TSG). Does anyone have more to add or have I missed something?"

The other brothers all agreed.

"Then let's call Marko up here and settle that part of it." Chung suggested.

"Yeah, then we go to dinner," Connie insisted.

CHAPTER 15
ANNOUNCEMENT TO
MARKO

Chung was given the initial opportunity, "Marko, we have some decisions to make and you are the middle man in most of them. Please sit, I believe you may need some support. Garland, would you like to do the introductions?"

Marko, "What do you mean? Who else do I have to meet?"

Garland, "Take it easy, Marko. You're going to be fine. Who was your Mother?"

Marko, "Eileen Fushier."

"What was her maiden name?

"Scott. Why?"

Garland continued, "What was your grandmother's name, maiden name also?"

"Her name was Maggie Cogburn Scott. What does that have to do with our deal?"

"Marko let me tell you a short story about Vernon Velgrove. He graduated from Harvard in 1912, went to Oxford for two years where he met a woman named Maggie Cogburn. He searched for Maggie Cogburn for eighty years. We have each spent a great deal of time and well over a million dollars trying to find her also. In a blink of an eye, her grandson has found us. Vernon would have been so proud of you, young man. It took guts to challenge the whole world and its terrorist ways. You see, when Maggie came to Vernon and told him she was pregnant, he hesitated just that one second. That proud Irish woman stomped off and disappeared. He never saw her again and could not find her or the daughter."

Marko interrupted, "What are you telling me?"

Garland continued, "Just bear with me, son. We think, in fact, we're fairly certain you are the grandson of Maggie Cogburn and Vernon Velgrove. We are asking that you have a DNA test to prove this, but we can see similarities in your visage and your actions. You are your grandfather's image, we all can see it. But to stop any questions you may have, please take the test. In the meantime we would like to continue with our plans.

Our plans are to set up the anti-terrorist group; you inherit Velgrove Industries, NY and will be trained by each of the brothers as we were each trained by Vernon Velgrove. You will be going to Egypt with Farimo to get a handle on that group while we setup the corps group. In three months you work with me at the Texas office. You will be introduced to our companies. Then you go to China and study the work there. After all that, you will be introduced to the world by Connie. In your new persona you will be the CEO of Velgrove Industries, NY, and will be responsible for the terrorist group. You will order who they attack."

Chung, "Marko, welcome to the corporation and the family Velgrove. Everyone grab a Champagne flute and let's toast."

Connie, "Then we go to dinner. We haven't all had dinner together in over ten years. This really is a stellar evening."

Farimo, "Here, here! To Marko."

Garland, "Here's to Maggie Cogburn, you finally found us Maggie."

Connie, "VV, you did good. DNA always comes through. You told me that but now I really believe you."

Chung, "Here's to Maggie Cogburn, Eileen, Marko and Vernon."

Nancy, "Here's to Marko."

Marko stood there staring at the Velgroves. He was truly shocked. After thinking he was all alone with no family, this was not something he could believe as true. For tonight, he was taken in hand and made 'welcome'. He even began to feel some emotion seeping through the haze of the past year. His professorship at Harvard was not a small fete. He had worked hard to accomplish his standing there. Giving it up to run a business did not seem like a trade-off he would choose, but for tonight he was caught up in the celebration and it did feel good to be wanted as family again.

They all got into the shore boat and went to dinner. They teased each other as brothers do. They drank too much because they knew they would have to face many questions and answers tomorrow, but tonight was a rare occasion. They were all having fun and enjoying their

Velgrove family.

Nancy and Marko sat together and looked at each other in that longing lover look. Connie saw it and said, "You two didn't get it on, did you?"

Nancy giggled. Uncle Connie was well known as the outspoken brother.

Marko looked Connie straight in the eye and said, "It's a good thing you guys came clean and told me the real story, I was ready. Nancy was really intriguing and I didn't know why."

Nancy hugged him and held his hand. She whispered, "Uncle Connie's the jokester, quick witted, outspoken and hot headed."

Connie paused, "Well, kid, maybe you did have a connection there. It's not verboten, you know, just not advised to have kids."

"Nothing happened. We just spent some time together. I guess she was sent to make sure I didn't bolt."

"Yeah, her father is pretty shrewd. He may have the most intricate business sense of us all."

As Connie turned and spoke to Farimo, Marko quietly asked, "Maybe you should tell me about the rest of the uncles."

Nancy whispered to Marko, "They are all really good men. They were raised by their mothers mostly, except for Garland, who had VV around all his life. Garland is a ladies' man somewhat. He likes to always have a beautiful woman on his arm. I think he is chauvinistic, but I'm a strong woman and know what I can do. Farimo is Egyptian, but you already know that. He works with the leaders in that country and has made good progress in alleviating starvation conditions in the back country where he owns property."

Marko asked, "What about your dad?"

"Oh, he's the best, but very intense. He expects me to accomplish everything he never did. He remembers everything. Don't ever expect him to forget, he just doesn't. His nickname growing up was elephant."

"I'll remember that," Marko replied.

They both laughed at Marko's pun. He squeezed her hand and looked deep into her eyes, wondering what would have happened if they were not family. He would take the DNA test quickly so he could pursue her further if he was not a Velgrove. As that thought danced through his head he leaned over and whispered, "You realize I may not be a Velgrove."

She leaned back and gave him an all over look, "No way. You look so much like my grandfather, you could be incarnate."

"Wow, I guess I need to see a picture."

CHAPTER 16
PLANNING, WHILE
RETURNING FROM
CATALINA

After dinner they walked back to the shore boat singing and mimicking *SINGING IN THE RAIN*. The four brothers danced along the street leading to the dock with arms around each other. They sang their father's favorite song, "Sweet Caroline" and Connie's choice, "My Brother."

Marko and Mei-Ling were walking arm in arm somewhat behind the brothers when Marko asked, "Who are the four men walking along the sidewalk, two on either side? Weren't they on the boat?"

"Sure, that one is my uncle Su Kung and the two over here are my cousins, Wu Kee a marine biologist and Sam Luk is the boat navigator. The other one over here is my mother's brother Shu Hi captain of the REGAL SONJIA."

"Why didn't they have dinner?"

"Oh, they were nearby. They are the caretakers when the brothers are together. They watch their back."

"You mean, a security team?"

Mei-Ling replied, "They're really just family, but if you prefer, you may call them security."

"I figured they were here because of me," Marko mused.

"You're not the only one who needs watching," she laughed. "Each of the brothers has had some close calls. Garland was hospitalized for three weeks one time due to an attack. That's when Connie started his company, Horizons International."

"I don't believe I saw that one in my information," Marko stated.

"Probably not, it's only used for high profile people. Connie had friends who needed protecting. He also goes to some exotic places and even though he's never had a problem during those travels, he is very adept at getting out of tight places. He did have something happen in Hollywood while coming home from one of his famous trips. I've heard a hundred stories of his journeys. Connie has a company which does portable up-link filming. If he goes someplace where he would not be allowed to take the film out of the country, he films while connected to a satellite which sends the video to his studio in Hollywood. The equipment fits in a few suitcases, depending on the terrain. These portable units are used by his crew and may be destroyed if necessary. Even the antenna folds down into an unrecognizable package. "

They reached the dock and all went aboard. Marko noticed there were a few other buff looking fellows and two women who came aboard also and disembarked on the boat with everyone. Could he have been so blind? He had not considered they would need security. Marko's world was whirling. He truly did not know how he would cope with his new identity.

As they boarded the boat Mei-Ling whispered, "I'll see you later."

He just said, "Okay."

Marko could not tell if he wanted the first woman he met, or if he really loved her. This was the nearest thing to love he'd experienced in years. Too bad they were cousins. Maybe they would just deal with it; after all they weren't real cousins. They were once or maybe twice removed. He couldn't wait to see her later.

The whole family sat in the stateroom talking and planning. Marko looked around with wonder that he was accepted into this group with no question. Then Mei-Ling walked into the room carrying a large picture. She sat it on the bar next to a mirror. She motioned for Marko to come there.

As he walked over and behind the bar, all conversation stopped. Everyone watched as Mei-Ling positioned the picture so Marko faced it and also could look at himself in the mirror. He looked at the picture and shook his head. It was a picture of Vernon Velgrove, age twenty. As Marko looked in the mirror he immediately thought, "It could be a picture of me at that age."

Out loud he said, "Good, Lord! I see what you mean."

The whole room laughed and continued talking, but Marko just couldn't stop looking at his grandfather's picture.

Connie, "Yeah, we need to get busy. I've been in touch with my Horizon people and we have a good body guard hook-up for him."

Garland sighed, "Don't forget what happened to me. You know it happens. Those people had been following me for months when they got me in the right place to hijack my car in Brazil."

Farimo continued, "I've set-up an office in Cairo with enough computers to run a whole business. The Input-Output software has not been installed. I'll take him to the Aswan and show him what his grandfather did there. We will proceed to the Oceanography and Fisheries in Alexandria where they investigate dynamics of food relationships in the southeastern Mediterranean coastal shelf ecosystem with the goal of outlining food webs leading to commercially important species. This ongoing investigation has established geographic and seasonal distributions of plankton organisms off Egyptian and Israeli coasts."

"That sounds like a great start for him. It'll show him the need for his analysis and maybe show his interests coincide with the company studies. Right now he's asking himself 'why should he change his career.' Even if he owns the New York Company he may not want to go there." added Chang.

"The old man always told me DNA comes through. This kid is too much like VV not to have some." Connie answered.

Garland added, "Let's give him a chance before we make too many predictions."

As they talked among themselves watching Mei-Ling charm Marko, Garland remarked, "She seems to have changed overnight."

The REGAL SONJIA was heading for San Pedro. They would arrive about 3:00am, if the weather stayed beautiful like this. Mei-Ling and Marko had walked out on deck talking about their grandfather where they watched from the foredeck as the boat left the harbor.

She wondered, "Will I ever see him again?" She couldn't decide whether to take Marko below and jump on him or pretend she didn't care.

She thought, "But, I do care. I care so much. Maybe I should just play it straight."

She said, "Marko, I care about you more than I have ever cared for anyone and I have only known you for two days."

"I feel the same, but this stuff with the brothers has me so confused, I can't make plans for my own life right now."

"If this makes you feel funny, I'm sorry, but I need to tell you how I feel, because I don't want to go through life like Grandpapa Vernon, always looking for the love of his life."

"My confusion has been multiplied by a thousand percent. I'm having so much trouble dealing with the tremendous upsurge in activity."

"I know. They're going to whisk you away soon

and I won't see you for awhile. That's okay, but you must know how I feel before they take you to Egypt or some place. I just thought you should know. I'm willing to meet you anywhere, anytime. Here is my cell phone number. Just call."

Marko grabbed her in a bear hug, "Honey, I love you too, but I just can't deal with it yet."

"Well, great! I pour my heart out and rejection!"

"Oh, don't say that. I would never reject you."

"You just did. "

"This is complicated!"

"Yeah, well I'll be at UCLA for another semester, and then as they say, I'm outa here."

"Mei-Ling, they have my life planned for the next year, maybe more."

"You will learn someday soon, the brothers want you to take your life back from them. That's the history of this family. Their father told them what to do until they told him what they would do."

"Are you ready to do that?"

"Marko, I'm still in college."

"Well, I'm new at this. My mother and father sent me out into the world and let me make my own mistakes."

"It's okay whatever you decide. After I finish my degree, I'll be gone. I will never call you. If you change your mind, my cell phone works and I will be waiting to hear from you, but only for the next four months."

Mei-Ling kissed him on the lips, walked to her cabin and went to bed.

Marko remained at the bow trying to sort through the many situations rolling through his brain. So many changes had occurred in these few days, since he had taken steps and walked into the Velgrove Industries, NY, Inc. offices. He was sure he cared for Mei-Ling, but quite frankly he was numb. He was a pretty analytical guy under any circumstances, but this situation was different and his feelings had been discarded completely since his mother and father disappeared with Supremenistas. Finally Marko went below, tossed and turned, sleeping fitfully.

Mei-Ling could not sleep, of course. She tossed and turned, made scenarios until 2:00am, then went back onto the foredeck to think.

Her father had not been pleased with the comments the other brothers made about either of his children. He had many plans for his daughter. His son was a disappointment. Since Sun Fo came to the U.S. he had ignored his father's directions. Connie seemed to understand Sun Fo better than his father. Chung supposed that was because Connie was a renegade also. Connie wanted to make films and VV never understood why. Chung tried to understand Sun Fo, but there were too many differences. His son was really a spoiled child who had never matured into the man he should have been. Raymond had. Chung had asked Raymond to assist his son in the NY office. Maybe his son needed to come home and learn the Chinese traditions. Dealing there would teach Sun-Fo the intricacies of the orient. Connie was right about one thing. Chung would turn the Xuanzhou, Xuancheng, Anhui, China company known as Industrial Rice and Grain, Pty. Ltd. over to his son. The negotiations this business required would challenge Sun Fo.

Chung was sitting in the boat's Main stateroom. After all the other brothers wondered off to bed he lingered there trying to solve problems concerning his son. Maybe this would help the other brother's businesses also.

As Chung left the room he glanced out the port hole and saw Mei-Ling standing on the bow leaning into the wind with her long black hair blowing. He walked to the foredeck. As he approached she turned and said, "Father, why are you up so late?"

"My daughter, why are you up so late?"

"I'm making decisions about my future, and you?"

"The same answer applies. I have decided to turn over the Industrial Rice and Grain, Pty. Ltd. to Sun Fo. Do you think he will take it seriously or do I need to hire an assistant to help him?"

Mei-Ling thought for a minute then answered, "Raymond will be with him, right?"

"Yes, as always."

"Raymond would be a much better businessman without my brother. He will keep that company from trouble, if possible."

"My daughter, you always have the right answer. I feel much better hearing your opinion, because it matches mine and I don't have confidence about decisions concerning your brother. I must have made all the wrong decisions for him in the past."

"Father, you made the right decisions. Charlie just insists on being belligerent and he always wants to do something different from others' plans. Do not blame yourself for Charlie's mistakes. He will continue to make mistakes. You know that. I don't have to tell you."

"My Mei-Ling, we don't talk enough. Maybe when you come home after your school is over we will spend time exchanging thoughts."

"I look forward to that time. Father you have been an excellent example for me and Sun Fo. I love you with all my heart and hope to make you proud."

Chung hugged her and said, "My daughter, I love you also and want only the best for your life."

The two Lees walked to the cabin door and said goodnight.

CHAPTER 17
MEI-LING RETURNS TO UCLA

About dawn the boat docked. Mei-Ling took all her things and quickly went to the taxi she had called and left for UCLA. Mei-Ling had her life well planned and everything had gone smoothly up until meeting Marko.

She had been a willful child and knew her own mind. When making decisions, she was a strong intelligent woman who went about her duties with confidence and diligence. As she traveled up the freeway towards UCLA, her heart was breaking. "I know it's silly, but I will yearn for Marko."

She called her chemistry lab partner as soon as she was in the dormitory. As she suspected, he was already in the lab writing his thesis. "I'll be there in thirty minutes with donut holes."

Kenneth Wong was suddenly in a good mood. She was back. The world was always more fun when Nancy was involved. He was on his laptop researching the next step of their qualitative chemistry class. He became absorbed and didn't hear Ahmed Nahbi enter the lab. When Nancy came charging in with the donuts and coffee, she said, "Ken, why didn't you tell me Ahmed was here?"

"Ahmed? I didn't know you were back there."

Nancy continued, "I would have brought you a coffee, but Ken here is deaf, you know."

Ahmed laughed, "Its okay, coffee isn't my favorite."

"Take some donut holes, here."

"Thanks," Ahmed said, "Where have you been?"

"Oh, I went to San Diego."

"I thought you were meeting your father in San Pedro."

"He was in San Pedro. I went to San Diego Yacht Club and was picked up by the yaa-chet."

"Yaa-chet? What's that?"

"You know, yacht, big ship."

"Oh I see a joke." Ahmed always missed the jokes.

Ken jumped in, "How much work, did you do during the last few days? I have the answer to ten of the twelve questions Dr. 'Quiznick' gave us to answer."

They all laughed at Ken's pun of the professor's name, Kisniack.

Nancy asked, "How did you know where I was going?"

Ahmed answered, "I heard you talking to Ken on Friday, why?"

"Oh, I just didn't remember seeing you here that day."

Ken chimed in, "It was probably one of those times Ahmed snuck in and sat there without saying anything."

"You always concentrate so totally, you never know what's happening around you," Nancy said.

"Well, let's get started here," Ken was always ready to study.

Nancy couldn't believe she had gone away two days and found love. Before she left, she had believed Ken was going to be her next lover. He was smart, dedicated and really good looking. All she could think about was Marko.

She couldn't even concentrate. As she tried to work she thought, "What a crock! I have totally screwed up my life."

CHAPTER 18
MARKO GOES TO EGYPT

Marko flew to Cairo on Tuesday. Farimo met him at the airport. As they drove Farimo explained about Vernon Velgrove's interest in archeology and the trips he made to Egypt in 1935 and again in 1952 after Gamal Abdal-Nasser pledged to control his country's annual flood with a giant new dam across the Nile River. They were going to the Abba Industries, Ltd. company river boat dock where the ADELLA MAR waited. In the next few days Marko would be told of his grandfather's help moving the statutes along the Nile and more history of Egypt and the Nile. Farimo talked the whole time they drove.

In the fifth century B.C., Greek historian, Herodotus, wrote "Egypt is the gift of the Nile." The Nile's annual flood cycle deposits several centimeters per century. Silt layers built the highly fertile Nile Delta in Egypt's northern area and the Nile Valley in the south. The Nile flood originates as Ethiopian highlands rainfall and melting snow of Uganda-Zaire border 'Mountains of the Moon'.

The Mediterranean ecosystem has been relatively

stable from time immemorial, but the Nile River's annual flood has been the most important event regulating the region's fertility. From the desert the great brown flood came pouring with its fertilizing effect on waters of the southeastern Mediterranean, or Levantine Basin. Two important events during the past one hundred years have happened in the Levantine Basin, opening of the Suez Canal in 1869 and construction of the Aswan High Dam in 1964.

The Aswan High Dam captured floodwater during rainy seasons and releases the water during times of drought. The dam also generates enormous amounts of electric power -- more than 10 billion kilowatt-hours every year. Although the construction of the High Dam has been an unquestionable asset to Egyptian agriculture and has benefited industry by providing cheap electric power, it has had comprehensive effects on the fertile silt and sediment movements. The sediments are now trapped behind the dam, a situation leading to severe erosion along the Egyptian coast. The dam has also had great impact on fertility of the coastal waters.

The fertilizing inflow effect of the nutrient-rich water during the flood season once resulted in exceptionally dense blooms of phytoplankton off the Nile Delta. This "Nile bloom" provided sustenance to sardines and other pelagic fishes. It also constituted a large source of detritus material, the products of organic decay, which forms a vital source of food for commercially valuable organisms such as shrimp.

Since 1965 when the High Dam became fully

operational, the Nile to Mediterranean flow has greatly diminished, although, dangerous floods in 1964 and 1973 and threatening droughts in 1972-73 and 1983-84 were limited.

Vernon Velgrove was more interested in the loss of Antiquities at Luxor and along the river. Temples at Philae and Abu Simbel would be under water. The Egyptian government appealed to UNESCO with whose assistance many monuments were dismantled and reconstructed on safer ground.

As Marko and Farimo surged up the Nile in the Abba Industries, Ltd. boat, ADELLA MAR, Marko was astounded seeing buildings and statues along the river. Marko had been rocked to sleep the previous night as the rush and gush of water lulled the tired travelers into a deep restful sleep.

Marko awoke rested and ready for the day before him. After breakfast, Farimo took him to see Hypostyle Hall then on to the Avenue of the Sphinxes or Sacred Way which once stretched the whole two miles from Karnak to Luxor Temple.

Farimo explained and described the antiquities they were seeing, "The most spectacular of the Karnak temples, Temple of Amun was dedicated to the Pharaoh Amun. The Karnak temple complex construction began in sixteenth century BC and continued into the Greco-Roman period. About thirty successive pharaohs added to the complex their personal touches, a new temple, shrine, or pylon and carved detailed hieroglyphic inscriptions. When the pharaoh Akhenaton abandoned traditional worship of Amun and took up the worship of Aten, the sun god, he built a temple to Aten at Karnak. But after his death, the Theban priests destroyed all signs of sun worship at Karnak and elsewhere. The Karnak temple complex covers one mile by two miles in area. There are over 25 temples and chapels in the complex."

He continued, "Necho II, King of Egypt circa 600 BC sent Phoenician sailors down to the Red Sea and along the coast of Africa. In the third year they returned through the Pillars of Hercules, which we know as Straits of Gibraltar, and reached Egypt through the Mediterranean Sea. According to many scholars, no other circumnavigation of Africa was repeated until Vasco da Gama rounded the Cape of Good Hope from the west two thousand years later, in the 15th century."

Farimo explained, "In the middle of the arid Egyptian desert lies one of the world's largest embankment dams called the Aswan High Dam, or Saad el Aali in Arabic. It captures the mighty Nile River in the world's third largest reservoir, Lake Nasser. Before the dam was built, the Nile River overflowed its banks once a year and deposited four million tons of nutrient-rich silt on the valley floor, making Egypt's otherwise dry land productive and fertile. But there were some years when the river did not rise at all, causing wide spread drought and famine. In 1952 Egyptian president Gamal Abdal-Nasser pledged to control his country's annual flood with a giant new dam across the Nile River. His plan worked. The Aswan High Dam captures floodwater during rainy seasons and releases the water during times of drought."

"Unfortunately, the dam has produced several negative side effects. Ninety thousand Egyptian peasants had to move. The rich silt normally fertilizing the dry desert land during annual floods is now stuck at the bottom of Lake Nasser. That's where our company's products come into play. Farmers have been forced to use about one million tons of artificial fertilizer as a substitute for natural nutrients once fertilizing the arid floodplain."

"About ninety-five percent of Egyptians live within twelve miles of the Nile. Since the dam was completed in 1970, Egypt's farmland has gradually decreased and today more than half of the soil is rated medium to poor. Enough rock was used in the construction of the Aswan High Dam to build seventeen Great Pyramids at Giza, one of the Seven Wonders of the Ancient World."

Marko relaxed in the yacht's main stateroom after the full day of site seeing. "Tell me what has happened to the economy in Egypt since Mubarak resigned."

Farimo winched, "Well, okay. But first a little background, during the 1990's a series of International Monetary Fund arrangements, coupled with massive external debt relief resulting from Egypt's participation in the Gulf War coalition, helped Egypt improve its macroeconomic performance. The pace of structural reforms, including fiscal, monetary policies, privatization and new business legislations, helped Egypt move towards a more market oriented economy and promoted foreign investment. Annual growth results averaged five percent annually, but the government largely failed to equitably share the wealth and benefits of growth failed to trickle down to improve economic conditions for the broader population. With the rebellion and Mubarak's step down, the Egyptian economy faces a rocky road to stabilize. It's a work in progress. Egypt has relaxed many price controls, reduced subsidies, reduced inflation, cut taxes, and partially liberalized trade and investment. Manufacturing has become less dominated by the public sector, especially in heavy industries, like steel and auto parts. The process of public sector reform and privatization has begun to enhance opportunities for the private sector. Agriculture, mainly in private hands, has been largely deregulated with the exception of cotton and sugar production. Construction, non-financial services, domestic wholesale and retail trades are largely private. According to the World Bank Country Classification, Egypt was promoted from the low income category to lower middle income category. Energy reform and food subsidies, privatization of the state-owned Bank of Cairo and inflation targeting are the most controversial economic issues."

"Farimo, we need to look at the Abba Industries, Ltd. options. Then we can optimize intermingling with the government and the other brother's companies."

"That's true Marko. I wanted you to have a good idea of the Egyptian back story as Connie would say. If you know what has gone on before it should be easier to plan for the future. A good deal of the income in Egypt comes from these antiquities. More money comes into this country through tourists than any other way."

"I can see why."

"You need to run an Input-Output sheet on my company, do you have your software or do I need to procure that from someone?"

"I have it."

"I thought you would."

"Farimo, I saw the computers at your office, let's get there so I can go to work."

"If that's your feelings, I'll order a helicopter to pick us up."

"Some hard work would do me a world of good. Let's get to the office and see what we have to work out there. Maybe we could continue this trip at the end of my stay here. At that time it will be more meaningful to the answers we can figure through the Input-Output analysis."

"We are only a few miles below Aswan Dam. The helicopter can pick us up in about two hours."

"Good I'll watch the birds over there wading in the shallows while you make arrangements for us. Thank you Farimo for doing this." Marko said to his uncle as he retrieved his cell phone and started making calls.

CHAPTER 18
MARKO GOES TO EGYPT

After three days of slogging through details of Abba Industries, Ltd., Marko was coming off his second 'all nighter' when Farimo arrived in the office saying, "Marko, don't you need some help. You can learn delegation or you can send yourself to an early grave trying to do everything yourself. VV would be appalled with your working all night like this. So come on, let's get some other people in here to do all this work. You're the supervisor, not the underpaid helper."

"Farimo, this is not just a little bookkeeping problem. This is taking all your records all the records established by the previous spread sheets of your area and comparing them. It's going well but I do need some help to complete the analysis."

"Who can we hire to help you?"

"There are at least three Harvard students who are good enough to work on this."

"Why don't you contact them and see what it will take to get them over here?"

"The good part is they don't even have to come here, we can do all this work online. I can set up a "cloud" account and we would be working together online."

"Marko, do it today. Don't wait. You will want to set up an office in Boston, owned by Velgrove Industries, NY, Inc., where the ongoing developments can be monitored in the future."

"That's a good idea. How do you do this so easily? I have always had to do everything alone."

"Yes, I can tell, Marko. We will teach you the Velgrove ways, delegation, communication, cooperation and a few more that come later."

"You guys are right. I really didn't know what I was getting myself into."

Farimo laughed. "You should have seen me and Chung when we started. Chung was graduating from Harvard when VV brought me to the U.S. continuing my schooling. It took awhile for us to find our footing, but it happened, just like it will happen with you."

"I don't have time to experiment though. I have to be ready for the anti-terrorist group."

"Why don't you investigate some other countries which have Input-Output studies? I happen to know that both Brazil and Australia are heavy into the macroeconomic studies."

"Farimo, that's a great idea. The International Input-Output Association or IIOA has lots of members in The Netherlands, Finland, Austria, Canada as well as United States. I have never joined because I thought a club wasn't something I needed to do, but cooperation at this point could help tremendously. That's something I need to do."

"Good! Before you leave, give Adella the names of people you want to reach. She will make an appointment for a time you specify or if you give her some details she will hire them on the telephone and set up your office for you. I can send her to Boston for a few weeks to get everything going smoothly, if you like. She is the best. You can trust her with everything."

"What about Nagilii?" Marko asked.

"He's not so good in math, but makes arrangements easy. I know you've been dealing with him. He's my son, but believe me, Adella, my wife, is best for this job in Boston."

"Could I meet her before you go?"

"Of course, Marko," answered Farimo. "I should have introduced you sooner. We just didn't have enough time for the niceties this week."

"Hey! Farimo, I figured you had family, I didn't realize I was already working with them."

"Of course, Marko, I have two daughters and three sons. My wife, Adella, is my best friend and partner."

"That's the Adella you want to go to Boston?"

"Yes. If that's alright?"

"Sure! Farimo! As you always say, of course." Marko suddenly felt tired and also relieved this impossible job would be made easier.

While in Chile with Doug Henry and Nissa, Marko had been in contact with the three students he mentioned earlier. He sat at his desk and picked up the phone to call the first, Malcolm Williamson. At this time

Mal would be home in bed, Marko hung up the phone and started writing an email.

"Malcolm, this is Marko Fushier. A woman named Adella will contact you in the morning about a job with me. I have a company now and am doing Economic Systems Research especially systems of innovative scientific and technological interdependencies. We plan an office in Boston and I also plan to contact Jerome Silva and Jeannette Rothman."

After three more emails he went to bed and slept soundly for the first time in months. The next morning he was rested and wrote one more email.

"Doralynn Reeves, how would you like to head up a crack corps of Input-Output researchers in Boston? You don't have to live there just visit occasionally. Your research into *Improved Calibration in Multisectoral Modeling* is the best. Adella Abba will contact you. Let me know when you can start."

Marko went to the office and presented Adella with the names of the three researchers and the company president Doralynn Reeves. He had outlined Macroeconomic Modeling research papers – *Inequality in Exchange: The Use of a World Trade Flow Table for Analyzing the International Economy* (applied to locales to be specified later); *Economic Integration: Systemic Measures in an Input-Output Framework* (to be applied Internationally later); *Labour Values, prices of Production and the Effects of Income Distribution: Evidence from Greece, and Denmark* (to be expanded to most other countries later); *Economic Modeling for Disaster Impact*

Analysis: Earthquake, Tsunami, Air Pollution, Volcanic Eruption, Water.

Marko met with Adella Abba in the conference room on the second floor of the industrial warehouse where Farimo had set up his office and computers. Adella was charming and knew all about Marko. He presented her with a typed dozier of all the potential new hires and the outline of what they should accomplish in the first few months of the business. They both were aware that the outline would change as soon as Marko went to Garland in Texas and The Netherlands where his largest business was located.

Adella read the outline and said, "I would like to discuss the research for following terrorists.

Marko responded, "Well we finally get down to the brass tacks."

Adella, "You mean the army brass must be included?"

Marko laughed, "I'm so sorry. I was using an Americanism. Please forgive me. I just mean, I'm relieved that someone is finally addressing that situation, besides me."

"Oh Marko, the brothers are very serious about addressing the terrorist situation. Over a million dollars has already been allocated for your project, five hundred thousand from each business. The Abba Industries, Ltd. is tracking the middle-eastern terrorists. I believe the Input-Output office will have oversight of terrorist's activities as they work on the money flow from country to country. Is that not correct?"

"Oh yes, Adella, it is correct."

"Then while I'm briefing the new employees in Boston, I'll alert them to the necessity of reporting such information to the office here at Abba."

"Excellent, excellent, Adella, Farimo said you were the best."

"It is always nice to be appreciated by ones' husband. No?"

"To tell you the truth he spoke very highly of your ability."

"Marko, we have lots of work to accomplish. May we start?"

They proceeded to work through the hiring process and when Adella saw it was the right time she called the prospective employees. As Marko listened he had to admire her dexterity in guiding the conversation in a business like direction and steering them away from the terrorists and other activities that might have sidetracked the potential employees.

At the end of the day they had hired five employees for Boston Macroeconomics Industries, Inc. The building had been leased, they had arranged a 'cloud' account, three of the statistical team would start work immediately from their homes and the office opened on Monday with ancillary personnel from a top employment agency. On Monday Adella would be in Boston to meet and greet and establish protocol. On the following Monday Doralynn Reeves would be available to run the office.

CHAPTER 20
INPUT-OUTPUT TEAM AT WORK

Doralynn Reeves arrived in the offices of Boston Macroeconomics Industries, Inc. at 7:00am on Monday morning. Adella was there waiting. That settled the 'who's in first' competition thought Dora. This woman means business.

Adella started talking first, "Ms. Reeves, I'm delighted to have you on board. Let's start with the project outlined by Marko Fushier. Do you have any further needs to complete that provision?"

"Please call me Doralynn. Actually, I would like to add one additional expansion to that outline as stated by Marko. *Alternative Approaches of Physical Input-Output Analysis to Estimate Primary Material Inputs of Production and Consumption Activities* as stated in the 2004 Economic Systems Research by Stefan Giljum and Klaus Hubacek is a reference that would be extremely helpful in fulfilling our present project. I believe I might get the cooperation of either one or both of those researchers."

"Doralynn, that's an excellent addition! You know

our budget. I leave it to your judgment whether to hire them or any other personnel. You will continually find essential requirements and the personnel coverage to accomplish the pertinent information we need. When we finish with our business' aspirations, we will have an auxiliary group offering information 'for sale' to outside organizations. Our companies will need intricate spreadsheets projecting possible product fabrication from the natural resources available. The macroeconomic information will also uncover political and problematic instances. That should be transferred to the Qatar Terrorism Office. I'm sure you will handle this smoothly."

"Thank you, Adella, for your confidence in me. That makes me much more relaxed pursuing the Trade Flow Tables analyzing world international economy."

"I understand there are three people working in remote locations, and five in-office employees working on the Flow Tables. Are there any ways to speed the production of these Tables? As usual we need it yesterday."

"Mostly, I've only worked under that type pressure. It's difficult to tell how much assistance we need at this time. That judgment will necessarily come as we get further into the data."

"Well then Doralynn, I leave the Boston Macroeconomics Industries, Inc. in your capable hands. I have a plane to catch."

"Adella, thank you for making this transition so easy. Is there anything I can do to make your trip go smoothly?"

"There is one thing. Tell me, where are the best sales in New York City today? Because you made everything move more smoothly, I'll have a few hours I may devote to shopping for clothes and special family items before I fly off to Cairo."

"It's done. Give me fifteen minutes to call my friend Gayle; she knows every sale in town."

"I won't be leaving for about an hour. I need to make some calls and clean up my mess in the store room. I dumped the bags I bought to take home in there."

"Good, the other employees will be arriving; I would like to introduce you to them."

"Thank you, Doralynn that would be nice."

"Now, I must call Gayle."

The two women laughed together. Only a few hours ago they were unsure of their positions, posturing to maintain their surety within the company. Doralynn made her phone call. Adella went to the store room to prepare her return to Cairo.

Doralynn had been surprised to hear from Marko. They had been at Harvard together. They were young and going for their Doctorates at the same time, and had become physically involved. They weren't in love but it was the next best thing. They accompanied each other on dates and outings. They studied together. Then she found the one.

She apologized to Marko for being so abrupt. He apologized for being less than perfect. They both agreed their affair was just that, an affair. They remained very good friends. Neither had brothers or sisters but continued to act like substitutes for those positions in the other's lives.

While Marko was in Chile, Dora got married and formed a close relationship with her husband, but Marko would always be her brother. She was also an Economics Professor, but had taken her job at NYU where Wassily Leontief moved after Harvard. She had spent a year at the Australia New Zealand National Bank in Sydney, New South Wales, Australia. She finally decided to marry and teach, so she returned to New York.

-----o-----

While Adella and Dora were setting-up the Boston Input-Output Office, Charlie was becoming more and more agitated, frustrated and dangerously upset. His buddies could hardly keep him calm enough to work. He made orders that couldn't be followed. Raymond was afraid Charlie was trying to bankrupt the business before he had to give it to Marko.

One Day in the second quarter Connie came breezing in called Raymond into his office and said, "Okay, Raymond, I know you know what's going on. I will not embarrass you by asking. I also know what's happening. We have to fix it. Charlie is making a fool of himself and his father cannot fix this because he's afraid of loosing Charlie. You must be his friend. I don't care what Charlie thinks of me so I'll be the 'bad guy' and somewhere up the creek he'll learn better."

"Mr. Kaulas, I appreciate your being candid. I don't know how to help you. Can you give me an idea?"

"Raymond, you are doing just fine. Just keep him from killing himself and others."

"Oh he'd never do that."

"I'm not so sure. I know he's been looking for someone to get rid of Marko. This cannot go on. We need to sidetrack him onto another project or give him so much work he can't think straight. Think about it and let me know if you have any ideas.

"Yes, sir. I will. Where should I call you?"

"Raymond, wherever I am Rosalyn always has my number. Have her dial and transfer back to you. That way no one will know you are dialing out. It will appear to be incoming."

"Thank you, sir."

Connie continued, "And, Raymond, don't wait too long."

While Marko finished his training in Egypt, Connie was planning a film with shooting locations in the French Alps. Raymond called Connie, "Connie, Raymond. Charlie has decided to hire a group of Tai Chi experts to kill Marko. They are going to arrive here in New York next week. I cannot stop him. Can you do something?"

"Let me go to the Office and contact the security corps. I will put a guard on Charlie and also on Marko. Marko will not be back in New York for awhile yet."

"Thank you, Connie."

"Don't let Charlie out of your sight. I will try to get him involved in my picture.   He might be a marvelous movie maker, who knows."

"He has mentioned your interest in him."

"If he will, I'll get him to help me on the *Alpine Events* movie. Keep in touch."

CHAPTER 21
MARKO GOES TO BRAZIL, BOLIVIA, PERU AND AMSTERDAM

Marko flew from Cairo to Amsterdam where he met Garland and his wife Phyllis. She never missed a trip to the diamond capitol, didn't spend money there, but always said, "I'm doing research. All my diamonds are bought by Garland."

Phyllis and Adella conducted operations of a small diamond mine with very little help. While Farimo's wife, Adella, and Phyllis were exploring a high mountain ravine on their Bolivian property, Adella saw a group of native women searching in a small mine. She mentioned to Phyllis the similarities to her mine in South Sudan. The two women spent several weeks camping in the mountains until they were able to gain the miner's trust.

As expected the women were mining diamonds, but had no sales outlet. Adella and Phyllis established a consortium with the Aymara women.

The Aymaras, Children of the Sun, were people

living in northern Chile, southern Peru and eastern Bolivia from time beginning. They ignored boundaries, were naturally easygoing, maintained their customs, language and beliefs but integrated into modern culture.

The diamonds were industrial quality usually, but occasionally a really beautiful specimen was unearthed. The Aymara women were able to live in homes of better quality and the men of the tribe continued to fish and farm as usual. They did rather enjoy the tools provided by the consortium.

Garland was introducing Marko to the companies making up the Velgrove Oil Company and the additional companies established as Velgrove International Industries, Inc. in countries outside the U.S.

Marko had analyzed Garland's holdings and knew they were 62.17% Gas and Oil, 14.78% Mining, 7% Retail and 5% Electronics leaving only 7.86% for all other categories – Data Management, Steel Production, Real Estate, Media, Communications, Animal Care Products, Trading, Airlines, Shipping, Food Production, Medical, Energy and Finance.

Garland said, "Let me tell you about Brazil. It has well-developed agricultural, mining, manufacturing and service sectors. Brazil's economy is larger than all other South American countries. Brazil has steadily improved its biodiversity. Its macroeconomic stability has built foreign reserves and reduced its debt profile by shifting its debt burden toward real denominated and domestically held instruments. In 2008, Brazil became a net external creditor and two ratings agencies awarded investment grade status to its debt. After record growth in 2007 and 2008, the onset of the global financial crisis hit Brazil in September 2008. Brazil experienced two quarters of recession as global demand for Brazil's commodity-based exports dwindled and external credit dried up. However, Brazil was one of the first emerging markets to begin a recovery. Consumer and investor confidence revived and GDP growth turn positive in 2010, boosted by an export recovery."

"Brazil's strong growth and high interest rates make it attractive for foreign investors. Large capital inflow over the past year has contributed to rapid appreciation of the currency and led the government to raise taxes on some foreign investments. President Dilma Rousseff has pledged to retain the previous administration's inflation targeting by the Central Bank, a floating exchange rate, and fiscal restraint." Garland hesitated then continued.

"Brazilian Exports include transport equipment, iron ore, soybeans, footwear, coffee, and autos. Their export partners are China 12.5%, US 10.5%, Argentina 8.4%, Netherlands 5.4%, Germany 4.1%. The import commodities are machinery, electrical and transport equipment, chemical products, oil, automotive parts and electronics. Brazilian natural resources include bauxite, gold, iron ore, manganese, nickel, phosphates, platinum, tin, rare earth elements, uranium, petroleum, hydropower and timber. It is the largest country in South America; shares common boundaries with every South American country except Chile and Ecuador."

Garland added, "Marko, you can readily see the export partners include China and Netherlands. That's mostly our products if you notice. Farimo has been making machinery and auto parts. Chung is involved in their electronics industry. If you notice the Brazilian national resources fit with these trading products. We have been able to find countries with resources we need to make the products we manufacture."

"Your businesses fit exactly with the economic tables we use."

"Well, son, we've been lucky. Really we've been selfish, since we only pick countries and products fitting our profiles. We haven't been adventurous with our companies. We only do what we know works already."

"Garland, that's just good sense."

"We do have some pretty good competition here. In Brazil, perhaps the only thing that's bigger than Eike Fuhrken Batista is Pão de Açúcar, the peak that dominates Guanabara Bay in Rio de Janeiro. 'Sugarloaf' mountain sits directly across from his tenth-floor office in the Praia do Flamengo building. Six years ago Batista swore he'd become Brazil's richest man. Now he is. With a net worth of $27 billion, two-thirds of that gained over the last 12 months, he's on his way to arriving at his latest goal, becoming the world's wealthiest."

"He's 53, has made a pile in resources and other services: mining (MMX), energy (MPX), logistics (LLX), real estate (REX), shipbuilding (OSX), tourism and entertainment. I asked him why all the x's in the names of his companies. He answered, "They're multiplying.""

But two-thirds of his fortune comes from a relatively new source--OGX Petróleo e Gas Participações, the oil-and-gas exploration company he founded in July 2007 and took public a year later."

"He's shrewd, but takes risks. He does have good timing and lot's a luck, but enough about him. Take him into consideration while you do the spreadsheets."

"Sure thing," Marko replied.

"Now, here is the information on the other South American countries where we operate."

"First, let me tell you about the part of Brazil I have seen," Marko suggested.

"Sure," Garland answered, "I'd love to hear about your trip through the Andes."

"When Doug Henry said he would help me find my mother and father, I was astonished and relieved at the same time. He knows so much about the countries here. His cabin is located near Barreal, Argentina. We traveled by train, bus, and any other means available for nine months searching for every bit of existing evidence we could find. The Supremenistas an anarchist group from northern Argentina left Buenos Aires headed for Cordoba being pursued by the Federales, so they took to the mountains and climbed the Sierras following the Incan trail. They went north into Bolivia and Peru and finally into Brazil and down the tributaries leading to the Amazon. They were able to escape unscathed because they were agile and never stayed in one place more than twenty-four hours. My mother got heart medicine for dad at least twice and probably many more times. The Supremenistas left them in Foz do Manoria. They were ill with fever and died within the week. The Indians buried them and that is where they will stay."

"We searched the Andes. We searched the archeological digs, where Doug had friends who took time off and helped us get to the right people who had seen the entourage proceeding through the countryside. No one got too close to those people. The local people were afraid of the armed soldiers who had the captives surrounded. Always there were a few days before the Federales arrived. They were just as brutal as the Supremenistas. So the local people trying to live their lives couldn't win."

Garland interrupted, "That's the way we make the most headway with our businesses. We respect and hire locals to run their own businesses and ours. Then we make a market to sell the goods produced. Pretty soon pride takes over and better products are created since it's theirs and they take pride in doing a better job.

Marko answered again, "That just makes sense."

"Let me finish with the other countries where we own property down here." Garland requested.

"Hold on! My brain's overloaded right now and I need this knowledge you've been telling me. You really are a fountain of knowledge, Garland. So would you mind if I record the rest of our conversation? You keep everything in your head. So many details and you just keep going."

"Well, Daddy always told me I kept too much in my head. But sometimes when you're making a decision, you can't wait to have somebody find a file for the details."

"Yeah, I know that can hold you up some."

Marko opened his briefcase and set a recorder on the table pointing it over toward Garland. "This should make it easier."

"Peru's natural resources include copper, silver, gold, petroleum, timber, fish, iron ore, coal, phosphate, potash, hydropower and natural gas. Peru's economy reflects its varied geography. It has an arid coastal region, the Andes further inland and tropical climate bordering Colombia and Brazil. Abundant mineral resources are found in the mountainous areas. Fishing Peru's coastal waters provide excellent results. The Peruvian economy grew by almost 6% per year during the period 2002-06, with a stable exchange rate and low inflation. Growth jumped to nearly 9% per year in 2007 and 10% in 2008, driven by private investment and government spending. But we faced world recession and fell to less than 1% in 2009. Growth resumed in 2010 at above 8%, due partly to a leap in private investment and continued high government spending. Peru's rapid expansion coupled with the government's conditional cash transfers and other programs helped reduce the national poverty rate by over 19 percentage points since 2002. Although underemployment still remains high, inflation in 2010 was within the Central Bank's 1-3% target range. Despite Peru's strong macroeconomic performance, dependence on minerals and metals exports and imported foodstuffs aligns the economy with fluctuations in world prices. Poor infrastructure hinders growth spread to Peru's non-coastal areas. A growing number of Peruvians are sharing in growth benefits despite President Garcia's trade and economic policies. Inequality persists, nevertheless, he remains committed to Peru's free-trade path. Since 2006, Peru signed trade deals with the United States, Canada, Singapore, China, Korea, and Japan, concluded negotiations with the European Free Trade Association (EFTA) and Chile, began trade talks with Central American countries and others. The US-Peru Trade Promotion Agreement (PTPA) established February 1, 2009, opened the way to greater trade and investment between the two countries. Rising world prices of food and fuel, together with strong domestic demands, are immediate concerns for 2011. Peru has continued to attract foreign investment. However, political disputes may hold up development of some projects related to natural resource extraction. They export copper, gold, zinc, tin, iron ore, molybdenum, crude petroleum and petroleum products, natural gas, coffee, potatoes, asparagus and other vegetables, fruit, apparel and textiles and fishmeal."

Marko was overcome by the details. "Garland, can you give me that in writing? Some form of report, would really help when I'm trying to put the numbers together on I/O spreadsheets."

"Well, I don't know where it is. You certainly can look at any of our books. I don't know how you work those spreadsheets."

"Garland, where is your central accounting center?"

"Well Marko, each company has its own bookkeeper. I coordinate the companies by product. All the oil and gas are lumped together so it's easier to ship the equipment around. Is that what you mean?"

"Not really. Where did all the information you're telling me originate?"

"I don't know. Pieces I read on an airplane, making trips across the countries watching what's happening. I just assembled the facts."

"Garland, I'm amazed. I could never remember all this. You have a complete brain full of details. I work with numbers every day. Do you want to continue?"

Garland nodded and started talking, He described the history and production numbers of Chile. Chile claims to have more bilateral or regional trade agreements than any other country. It has 57 agreements, not all of them full free trade agreements. Chilean exports include copper, fruit, fish products, paper and pulp, chemicals and wine."

"Rescuing the minors was on all televisions," Marko commented.

"Yeah, but television only saw the rescues there was so much work done by everyone. Even the local people worked 24/7." Garland said.

"Now, Bolivia where we have the most property to develop is one of the poorest and least developed countries in South America. After higher prices for mining and hydrocarbon exports produced a fiscal surplus in 2008, the global recession in 2009 slowed growth. Nevertheless, Bolivia recorded the highest growth rate in South America that year. During 2010 an increase in world commodity prices resulted in the biggest trade surplus in history. However, a lack of foreign investment in the key sectors of mining and hydrocarbons and higher food prices pose challenges for the Bolivian economy. Natural resources include tin, natural gas, petroleum, zinc, tungsten, antimony, silver, iron, lead, gold, timber and hydropower."

Marko listened and analyzed the situation. After a pause he said, "Garland, this is so complicated, I will hire analysts in both The Netherlands and Brazil. There is a well known Professor Oosterhaven, University of Groningen, The Netherlands who is actively involved in research. He will help me find the appropriate person. I have collaborated with Erik Dietzen from the same university. They are both involved in the International Input-Output Association."

"That sounds like a good plan. I understand the Analysis Group has already been set up in Boston. Can they supervise these people also?"

"Sure. Adella managed that set-up smoothly."

"Yeah, Adella is a gem, heh, heh. She loves gems, diamonds and anything shiny. Farimo really lucked out there. She is one in a million."

"She sure is. She already saved us a million dollars during the set-up."

CHAPTER 22
MARKO GOES TO CHINA

Chung Kee Lee met Marko Fushier at the Hong Kong airport. As they drove Lantau Highway eventually entering the under ocean tunnel leading to Aberdeen, Chung explained the interaction of their company with the Chinese government demands.

Marko was astonished. Coming out of the tunnel into the remarkable tall buildings was breath taking. The bright air and swirling breezes were so refreshing. "This place is amazing, Chung," Marko commented. "Where do you live?"

"I live in the high rise on the top of that hill, the one overlooking the ocean where the QUEEN ELIZABETH-I sank. The harbor has changed. The opening of Hong Kong Airport at Chek Lap Kok in 1997 took the QE-I and left only a portion in the seabed."

Marko asked, "Was that sunk just before WWII?"

"No. In 1972 while undergoing refurbishment, she caught on fire under mysterious circumstances and capsized," Chung replied. "This place has a rich historical background. For centuries China stood as a leading civilization, outpacing the rest of the world in the arts and sciences, but in the 19th and early 20th centuries, the country was overwhelmed by civil unrest, major famines, military defeats, and foreign occupation. After World War II, the Communists under Mao Zedong established an autocratic socialist system. While ensuring China's sovereignty, it imposed strict controls over everyday life and cost the lives of millions of people."

"Since the late 1970s China has moved from a closed, centrally planned system to market-oriented playing a major global role. In 2010 China became the world's largest exporter. Reforms began with phasing out collectivized agriculture and expanding to include gradual price liberalization, fiscal decentralization, increased autonomy for state enterprises, creation of a diversified banking system, development of stock markets, private sector rapid growth and opening foreign trade and investment. China has implemented reforms gradually. Recently, China has renewed support for state-owned enterprises in sectors it considers important to 'economic security,' explicitly looking to foster globally competitive national products."

Marko commented, "We had trouble getting 'real' information due to the secrecy of the government economists."

"Yes, we've had people in government who tried to keep the ancient beliefs of disassociation with the outside world. However, after 1978, Mao's successor Deng Xiaoping and other leaders focused on market-oriented economic development. By 2000 output had quadrupled. For much of the population, living standards have improved dramatically and room for personal choice has expanded, although political controls remained tight. Since early 1990s, China increased its global interaction and now participates in international organizations."

Marko asked, "Does Chinese currency hold its value in your trading?"

Chung continued, "It has held value. It was tightly linked to the US dollar for years, in July 2005 Chinese currency revalued by 2.1% against the US dollar and moved to an exchange rate system referencing an assortment of currencies. From mid 2005 to late 2008 cumulative appreciation of the renminbi against the US dollar was more than 20%, but the exchange rate remained virtually tied to the dollar from the onset of the global financial crisis until June 2010, when Beijing allowed resumption of a gradual appreciation."

"How did you make that transition of the devaluation?" Marko asked Chung.

"The economy restructuring and resulting efficiency gains contributed to more than tenfold increase in GDP since 1978. Measured on a purchasing power parity (PPP) basis that adjusts for price differences, China in 2010 stood as the second-largest economy in the world after the US, having surpassed Japan in 2001. The dollar values of China's agricultural and industrial output each exceed those of the US. China is second to the US in the value of services it produces. Still, per capita income is below the world average."

"The Chinese have endured for centuries by ignoring those in charge of the government. It seems like Chinese just ignore their capturers. So many dynasties have come and gone and people have kept on running their lives and family in the same way for centuries," Marko commented.

"The Chinese government faces numerous economic challenges," Chung continued. "You're right, economic development has progressed further in coastal provinces than in the interior where people don't welcome changes. Approximately 200 million rural laborers and their dependents have relocated to urban areas to find work. One consequence of the 'one child' policy, China is now one of the most rapidly aging countries in the world. Deterioration in the environment, notably air pollution, soil erosion and the steady fall of the water table, especially in the north, is another long-term problem. China continues to lose arable land to erosion and economic development. The Chinese government wants to initiate energy production from sources other than coal and oil, focusing on nuclear and alternative energy development."

Marko entered the discussion with, "We could take lessons from their energy methods."

"In 2009, the global economic downturn reduced foreign demand for Chinese exports for the first time in many years, but China rebounded quickly, outperforming all other major economies in 2010 with GDP growth around 10%. The economy appears set to remain on a strong growth trajectory in 2011, lending credibility to the stimulus policies the regime rolled out during the global financial crisis. World leader in gross value of agricultural output; rice, wheat, potatoes, corn, peanuts, tea, millet, barley, apples, cotton, oilseed, pork and fish, China also is the world leader of industrial output gross value: mining and ore processing, iron, steel, aluminum, and other metals, coal, machine building, armaments, textiles and apparel, petroleum, cement, chemicals, fertilizers, consumer products, including footwear, toys, and electronics, food processing, transportation equipment, including automobiles, rail cars and locomotives, ships, and aircraft, telecommunications equipment, commercial space launch vehicles and satellites."

"The Velgroves have oil and gas production near Yingkou, but our inland locations are more productive." Marko added, "Where is most of the computer production done?"

Chung responded effusively, "I'm so glad you are with us, Marko. Your knowledge brings intelligence to our businesses. My son has refused to acknowledge you so far. I must apologize for his rudeness."

"Chung, I've been so busy. It has been impossible to see everyone. I wanted to talk to your son, but he was never available. Is there a problem?" Marko asked.

"I am afraid there may be eventually. I must protect the company and keep my son traveling in the proper path while developing the companies."

Marko thought the conversation sounded somewhat

strange, but so engrossed in the Chinese story he didn't pay attention to Chung's warning.

Chung continued, "China's natural resources include coal, iron ore, petroleum, natural gas, mercury, tin, tungsten, antimony, manganese, molybdenum, vanadium, magnetite, aluminum, lead, zinc, rare earth elements, uranium and the world's largest hydropower potential. The natural hazards are frequent typhoons, about five per year along southern and eastern coasts, damaging floods, tsunamis, earthquakes, droughts and landslides."

"China is the world's fourth largest country, after Russia, Canada, and US. Mount Everest on the border with Nepal is the world's tallest peak. Vernon was always fascinated with the diversity of China. When he came here as a young archeologist he was fascinated with the antiquities found. In 1915 VV visited the Astana graveyard in the Turfan Oasis, a valuable information source of daily life along the Silk Road. He spent seven years excavating in China. Astonishing finds from the Turfan Oasis revealed Silk Road history. Then he negotiated with the Soong banking group who controlled the financial industry for over a century in China. Spreadsheets like you produce were unknown here. There were analysts hired by the Soong Bank who simulated Input-Output but, I was never privy to that information."

"Well Chung, you will have all you can use now," Marko replied. "Japan's Keio University has a good department of Macroeconomics. If you cannot find a

Chinese university with departments of Economics we may use the Keio students. At Harvard there is one Chinese student, Mat Ho, who possibly would work with us."

"Marko, the Macroeconomics is going smoothly and you have done an excellent job setting-up and running the Research Analysis office, but that is not the focus. We will concentrate on running your company, Velgrove Industries, NY, Inc. It is important you become acquainted with the interaction of the four brothers with the New York office. That office has always made decisions we used to transition our companies into other countries and other industries."

Marko was astounded at Chung's seriousness and paid attention to his every word.

"I am eighty-one years old. I will not be here forever. My daughter, Mei-Ling, was supposed to take the business when she graduated UCLA in June, however in the last six months she has become unreliable and has even disappeared from her father."

"Chung, what happened to her? What do you mean, she disappeared?" Marko asked.

"We saw her in June at the graduation. She should have come to Hong Kong in a few weeks. I thought she was taking a vacation week. She worked very hard on her thesis. She never arrived in Hong Kong. I cannot find her. I have Connie's Horizon group looking, but they have not come up with any further information."

Marko was crushed by this information and could tell the father in Chung had completely taken over.

"Chung, I have not heard a word from her. I thought we would keep in contact, but I got lost learning my new job, well jobs."

"She would not have disappeared like this; I suspect she must be kidnapped."

"Chung, what happened when you went to the graduation?" Marko asked.

"She was happy, proud and introduced her mother and me to all her friends. She invited her friends to China for a visit. She gave out her new cards stating PhD on them. She was as always."

"We must find her. I have thought of her every day since she left." Marko admitted.

"Marko, maybe you and I are not the ones to follow the trail, since I see you are as emotionally involved as I. Let's call Connie and get him personally involved. I only contacted his company. I did not talk to Connie."

"Good, Chung, as soon as we get to the office, I will call him."

"You will have appointments almost every moment you are here. Tonight is going to be a family night. Nila, my wife is expecting you for dinner and you are staying in the hotel across the street from our condo. By then I will have called Connie. Please read the documents I included in the briefcase provided at the airport."

"Thank you, Chung. All the Velgroves seem to be extremely well organized, so was my mother. I guess DNA really is important. I would have argued with that a few months ago."

"Connie always argued with VV about DNA being strong suit of a person's make-up."

Chung dropped Marko at the hotel and requested he arrive at 6:00pm for dinner. The trees along the sidewalk in front of the hotel smelled of a perfume hard to describe. As he walked in and turned to wave goodbye, he saw Chung was already instructing the driver to leave.

After unpacking in the hotel he sat in a hot tub and read the material Chung had provided. Marko was amazed at the documents. Each page brought another indication of the businesses interacting. By dinnertime he had made it through half the documents and had dozens of questions for Chung, Farimo, Garland and Connie. Marko had not had time to think, since he started this trek through the Velgrove industries. He saw a sign in the hotel lobby advertising yoga and meditation. On a whim, Marko turned to the desk and asked the clerk to arrange for the yoga and meditation coach to come to his room in the morning at 5:00am. He had always wanted to learn meditation and he supposed yoga went along with it.

Chung's wife, Nila was charming. She had arranged an evening of food and entertainment. Nila showed Marko her art work. She was a famous oriental artist as well as poet. She engraved her poetry on scrolls and painted her pictures on silk. As they returned to the living room a string quartet had set up in one corner and was playing quiet music for dinners. She took Marko directly to the dining room where Nila was astonished to see her son.

"Sun-Fo, I am so very happy to see you here. Please have you met Marko Fushier?"

Sun-Fo Lee was at dinner with ten other guests. It was the first time he had actually met Marko. He arrived with an entourage of body guards and the most beautiful woman Marko had seen, since Mei-Ling left him on the boat coming back from Catalina. Sun-Fo held court during dinner, dominating the conversation about world events and current social situations. He asked Marko point blank several times what he thought about these subjects.

Marko had been so overloaded working he had no time to pay attention to events and said so to Sun Fo. After dinner he made a point of talking to Marko.

"Mr. Fushier, I am S.F. Lee."

"I am so very glad to meet you finally. I wanted to ask you about the New York Office." Marko said.

S.F. looked at Marko questioningly, "Why is that?"

"Maybe I'm wrong, but weren't you there for almost a year?" Marko continued, "I was sure that's what I was told by the personnel department. I've had so many details thrown at me in the last six months, maybe I misunderstood."

"Oh, I spent much of my time there, but I have so many businesses I had little time for Velgrove Industries. I am more involved in the financial businesses, not manufacturing or produce." S.F. replied. "When you run out of money, you will know what I do."

"That will be educational, I'm sure."

Marko knew something was very wrong in this conversation, but he couldn't put his finger on it. He made a mental note to check when he returned to the New York Office.

Raymond saw S.F. talking to Marko and moved across the room and whispered to S.F. that they had previous arrangements. They started moving to leave. Nila cried as her son said goodbye. She loved him so and he had not been for a visit lately. S.F. and Raymond moved on toward the door with their entourage. As they left it seemed as if a vacuum was formed. Chung walked over to Nila and put his arm around her waist. She laid her head on his shoulder and they both sighed.

Nila was the granddaughter of Chi-Ming Sook wife of a famous revolutionary and banking family member. Nila had been raised in Missionary Schools by strangers. She had rarely seen her family and knew the longings it caused. When she met Chung Kee Lee and found his father had come back to find him, she was so impressed. Chung was wanted. His father had cared about him. That was so impressive to Nila that nothing else mattered.

Chung did not mention work or Mei-Ling during the evening. When Marko returned to his hotel, there was a call waiting. It was Connie.

"Hey kid, what's happening over in the orient?"

"Well I only know what is fed to me. They feed me info 24/7 with a little food in between," Marko replied.

"Well, we have a problem. Nancy has disappeared

and nobody knows where she is. I went to her dormitory myself. Her chemistry partner was the last to see her. He seemed upset because he was jealous of another kid who was 'coming on to her' he said. Did you hear anything after she left?"

"No. I kept thinking I would contact her when I had time, but you know how that went down," Marko answered.

"We did get some information about the Volkswagon that blew, oh, that's right. You didn't come to the boat in Los Angeles. As Garland went over the Vincent Thomas Bridge in San Pedro a Volkswagon blew almost beside him. The police found some gang kids under the bridge with detonation equipment. The real story is they were very rich. They had much more money than they should have. They easily admitted that a middle-eastern looking kid paid them to set up the VW explosion."

"Connie, what does this have to do with Nancy?"

"The only connection to Nancy is the other chemistry partner, who just happens to be Lebanese is the one her real partner was jealous of and is also missing from the university."

"You may be taking a big leap there, Connie," Marko added.

"Yeah, but there are no coincidences you know. It's too close, too close."

"What can I do?"

"You can keep your nose to the grindstone and get to Velgrove Industries NY, Inc. as soon as possible. We could get you lined up with the Anti-terrorist Group and you can take over finding your cousin."

"Is the Anti-terrorist Group ready to deploy?" Marko asked.

"They will be in another month. They're going great on the training and we have them working 24/7. Now they will start on a real problem. The research is everything."

"You can't go until we get them cleared by the World Bank or UNESCO or someone."

"Marko, that's why I need you to finish with Chung and get here. You are the only one to do that job. I'll be waiting for you in Los Angeles. You need to get here quicker than possible." Connie retorted. "After you talk to Chung tomorrow call me."

Connie hung up the phone, but Marko looked at it for a few minutes before replacing the cell phone in his pocket and starting to read the packet locked in his briefcase. At 3:00am, he went to sleep and woke promptly at 4:45. He quickly showered and was ready for the five o'clock yoga and meditation coach.

-----o-----

Sun-Fo Lee moved to Shanghai after his Uncle Connie asked him to go on a filming expedition up the Matterhorn. As it turned out, Charlie wasn't quite as brave as he had imagined. After sliding around on the ice for awhile he had given up and requested to go home. Connie took him aside and had a talk, "Charlie, you are no longer working at the New York office, but you already know that. You need to return to Shanghai and run your business there."

After Charlie left Connie, he decided to go to Macau for a little vacation. The Sands Macau Hotel welcomed him as a high roller and he lost a half million dollars at the crap tables. He became personally acquainted with the owner who needed someone to front a project in Shanghai and Shantau. They made a deal to open a casino in Shanghai. Charlie, or his new identity S. F. Lee, went to Shanghai and found he had a knack for money. He hired some local guys for the casino security and as time passed he fumed and planned until he had a scheme working for the elimination of Marko Fushier. Time would be on S. F.'s side. He would wait and find the perfect time to revenge his heritage.

-----o-----

Mei-Ling was not getting along as well as her brother. After graduation night and the family left, the next day she was packing and finishing postponed chores when the telephone rang. It was Ahmed Nahbi saying they were having a celebration at Moe's Bar down the street and all the foreign students would be there since they had to return home in a few days. She asked if he had invited Ken and Ahmed said sure he had. She finished the chores and went to the bar around 7:00pm. Seeing all her friends were there already and drinking heavily, she decided she should catch-up.

The next thing she knew she was feeling hung-over and groggy on an airplane in first class with Ahmed. He kept giving her tea and soda. She kept falling asleep. She vaguely remembered changing planes somewhere on the trip. She felt high. She had never taken drugs but supposed this was the way it felt.

Before they landed the last time, he took her into the lavatory and put a burka on her. They deplaned in a small airport. There was very little commotion or immigration checking. They were met by a driver in a black Mercedes van and whisked through the small city. Ten or fifteen miles into the countryside they turned into an estate with a large house and several smaller houses beside it. She was locked in a room for five days before Ahmed came in and talked to her. She was fed strange food and could only talk to two other women. After five days he informed her that she was being held for ransom, but her father had said he would not pay so she could pay for it herself by working with the jihad and helping them capture the infidels in Sudan who were feeding the revolting people there.

He said, "I must prove to my family you are compliant and will help us or they will kill you."

"Ahmed, I will do whatever I need to do to convince your family. Why don't you let me call my father? He will cooperate with you."

"No! I must prove first."

That day he marched her into the main room of the big house and proceeded to beat her until she could no longer stand. She recuperated for a few days and then he did it again. His family laughed and said he was not hitting hard enough. The other women in the locked room bathed and bandaged her wounds. They tried to convince her he would stop soon, but he didn't. She became listless and thought she would die soon. When Ahmed went away to train for the jihad, his three brothers stopped laughing and started taking turns raping her. When he returned he was very angry. He took her to the back house, raped her and stuffed something into her vagina.

He told her, "This is your fault. You let them have you. You are a marked woman and I should have you stoned in the square. I will take you with me to the Sudan. I just put a bomb in there and you will die if you take it out."

That night she lay in the bed crying and wishing she had not been so hard on Marko. He probably didn't know she was missing yet, but he would. Then she started to hypothesize. If I could let him know, would he come get me? I know he would. She knew it was unrealistic, but she had nothing else to hang on to. So she played the game of Marko riding through the door on a horse to carry her away. When Ahmed beat her again, she stared him in the face and didn't blink. He probably realized he had pushed her too far, but he didn't care. He was having the time of his life. He had her exactly where he wanted her. She was his slave and she would always be. The rest of the family finally lost interest and looked on her as a waste. She couldn't work or contribute so she was ignored.

She started going to the market with the kitchen help. She picked the best fruits and vegetables. The other women appreciated her choices and knew she had been mistreated. They tried to make her more comfortable without annoying the other members of the household. Slowly the beatings became less frequent. She spent most of her time fantasizing that Marko was just down the street and would arrive soon.

CHAPTER 23
MARKO GOES TO NEW YORK

Chung quickly finished the presentation of his various Hong Kong companies and sent Marko to Connie, who was ready to move and on several levels, but first they would go to dinner and have a relaxing weekend.

After months of traveling constantly, Marko was glad to be in a home. He could finally relax and think. The Boston office was running smoothly. He took a leave of absence from Harvard Business School. This delegation thing was really working. He owed Farimo for teaching him that trick of the trade. The only worry was where was Mei-Ling?

Connie was having a good time presenting his life. Wearing gray khakis, worn slippers and his signature wire-rim glasses Constantine Koulas, Hollywood producer, enjoyed showing his Malibu beach home to his nephew. Connie slipped easily into his role as the entertainer. They walked on the beach, watched the surfers taking rides on the breaking waves, watched the light changes at sunset and watched the long legged birds taking the waves. After walking barefoot in the sand, they returned, rinsed the sand from their feet and were sitting in the glass enclosed living room watching the day's last fragment slip away behind the earth's curve.

"You want to see my collection?" Connie asked Marko.

"Sure, if I don't have to move. The rolling crash of waves outside is lulling me into a sense of sanctuary."

Sipping champagne from a wineglass, Connie said, "I'll just point. I have a worthwhile collection spread throughout my homes in Thessalonica, Paris and of course here. Paul Klee said 'Art does not reproduce what is visible; it makes things visible.' I have paintings by Picasso, Van Gogh, Kandinsky, Matisse, Boccioni, Van Zandt and this small sculpture is by Rodin."

The cry of an infant upstairs pierced the quiet. Connie disappeared and reemerged with his 9-month-old son, Shimon Alexander and his wife, Amanda, a petite blonde from Tasmania who once ranked among the world's best women tennis players.

"Two generations of Shimon," Connie laughed, nodding at a framed photo of Shimon Peres, Israel's president and a close friend, cradling the baby.

"Bringing peace to the Middle East is most important to me," Connie said, suddenly serious. "I think we can do it, but not today. That is a subject for another time. Today we just simmer in the heat."

"Connie, I'm so relaxed, it would take me twenty-four hours to recover enough to really care about the middle-east."

"That reminds me, I must make a phone call. Joseph, bring me the phone."

Amanda took the baby, Shimmy, and walked out to the beach.

The house boy, Joseph, responded, "Yes sir, it's just beside the couch, let me get it for you."

"That's okay, Joseph, I see it now."

Connie proceeded to call an assistant at International Films, Inc., his production company, and asked to be connected to some people who had discussed his investing in Sony Pictures previously in the office. Connie dialed and talked on speaker phone.

"I'm really very interested in this deal," he said, "I know maybe I didn't sound that way earlier but I've been thinking about it. Jesse mentioned Miramax might be for sale as well, for $600 million or so. Let's look at that one, too. Ask if they would be willing to compensate for the new picture ready to be released."

The assistant on the phone answered, "That shouldn't be a sticking point, and it will only make it a better deal for them."

"Please get back to me on this as soon as possible, remember we are in a fluid situation right now, maybe next month we won't be."

Connie a creative, ferociously focused entrepreneur, with a net worth estimated at $3.6 billion, coming from movies, fertilizer, weapons systems and commodities. At age 56 he's far from retired. After the Mumbai bombings in late 2008, Connie founded Horizon

International, a security company, to help protect friends like Jamsetji Nusserwanji Tata, owner of the Taj Hotel, where the terrorists struck. Connie well connected in Hollywood, Europe and Israel, exploited his relationships to further his social and political interests, as well as his business goals.

Often he discussed the 100-plus films he produced since launching the privately held International Films, Inc. in 1983. Today, he claimed, it grossed in excess of $1 billion a year and has been responsible for recent box-office hits *The Dust over Israel*, *Mr. & Mrs. Jones*, *Barbella Returns* and the latest release *Tasmania Race*.

Connie grew up with Garland, their mother Katy Koulas and Vernon Velgrove. He was sent to boarding school, went to college at USC where he studied film making, but Vernon insisted he study business administration in Geneva. Connie took over an Israeli company which was barely surviving and within two years had turned it into a diversified corporation with business in agriculture, animal health products, plastic, fiber optics and pharmaceuticals. He expanded to Iran, Turkey and Greece.

Marko knew some of Connie's history but as they relaxed drinking Champagne and listening to the waves he thought to himself, "This life might not be as bad as I first thought." Working with the Velgrove Brothers was daunting at best, but Connie had just revealed the other side. All the Velgrove Brothers had beautiful homes, some had several, like Garland and Phyllis with homes in Amsterdam, Bolivia and Texas and Connie with ocean views in three countries.

As they sat listening to the waves, the phone rang. "Hello, that's fast."

Marko could only hear one end of the conversation. Connie commented, "Well, that little shit! He just had to do it. I'll handle it in some unique way. Thanks for the quick info." Connie turned to Marko and said, "Someone already bought the Sony Studios."

Marko couldn't get too involved. He just said, "Too Bad, you could have done a lot with that property."

"Yeah, but it's really high maintenance. Maybe I'm lucky I didn't get it."

"This is so comfortable I don't really care about anything right now." Marko commented.

Amanda returned from the beach with Shimmy. They played with the baby, but he was ready for his bath and supper so the nanny took him away waving and laughing.

Amanda sat and said, "Marko, you look tired. Let's make our evening here; we don't need to go out to dinner. I'll stir up something."

Connie responded, "Now Darling, we planned on going to the Saddle Peak Lodge, we have reservations for eight."

"Well, if you insist. I know how you like that place. I'd better get dressed, if we're going there." Amanda said as she rose and left the room.

Connie laughed, looked around the door in the hallway then said, "She is such a dear. Her tennis took so much time she never learned to cook. Besides she's a proclaimed vegetarian. You'll love this place."

"I'm sure I will. What have you found out about Mei-Ling?"

Connie looked puzzled and asked, "Who?"

Marko responded, "Nancy, Mei-ling Lee, you know, your niece."

"Oh, oh. The Qatar Group is analyzing every bit of information available since her graduation. We have proven she left Los Angeles with Ahmed Nahbi. They are probably in Lebanon, but we don't have much information coming out of there lately."

Marko sat up and exclaimed, "How could she be there? What would she do there?"

"Marko, there has been no contact. We are surmising their destination. You were really taken by her, weren't you?"

"Connie, I will admit. Yes, I love her. I've thought of her every day since the dinner in Catalina. We agreed to go our own ways and I was trying to keep my promise to her."

"Well, it looks like she went way off the track."

"Oh, Connie, don't say that. She is immensely trustworthy you must know that, don't you?"

"Not really."

"She worked for her father and she went to school, she knows nothing about the real world. Someone took advantage of her good heart. I'll bet on that."

"I hope you're right. I also hope we find her soon. Chung is having a difficult time believing we are working on this diligently."

"I understand how he feels. I will talk to him daily when I get to New York. You need to keep me abreast of the progress or if you'd rather, I'll go direct then you won't have to baby sit this process."

Connie laughed, "VV got through to you in a big way. You are so much like your Grandfather it's scary. He always told me DNA was what made the family businesses run so well together, but I argued with him all the time on that subject."

Marko, Amanda and Connie went to dinner at the Saddle Peak Lodge for the best steak Marko had ever tasted and wine to write home about. The weekend went quickly and when Marko caught the 'redeye' to New York Sunday night he felt rested and part of the family. All these brothers treated him like a son. He still missed his mother and father. He would always miss them, but four other people were making little inroads into his emotional psyche and he wasn't complaining.

When Marko arrived at Velgrove International Industries, Inc. he hesitated at the front door. He had not been back since leaving the letter for Chung Kee Lee threatening exposure. Now he was walking into his business. The exposure threat was probably a non-sequitur at this point. He grabbed the door and swung it open to the receptionist he had talked to before.

She said, "Hello Mr. Fushier. How are you today, Sir?"

"Please tell me your name so I'm not at such a disadvantage. Oh, I see your badge, Rosalyn."

"Yes, sir, everyone must wear one."

"Rosalyn, do you know why I'm here?"

"Yes, sir, Mr. Lee and Mr. Kaulas briefed us all on Friday."

"Good. I will need a list of employees, a list of their expertise and the length of their employment with their salary. I realize you will obtain this information from the HR department. Just notify them and have them bring that information to my office."

Marko spent the morning interviewing employees of the NY office. He wanted to know who would work with him and who would soon leave of their own accord. In the afternoon he started to make assignments. Projects were soon in full swing as he kept in touch with Connie, Chung, Farimo and Garland. In the first few months they talked five or six times during the day. Also, he was in constant contact with the Boston Analysis Group (BAG) and was introduced to the Qatar Terrorist Analysis Group (Q-TAG).

They zeroed in on a Lebanese al Qa'eda group training near Baalbek. Part of their training included an attack on the soldiers cleaning up unexploded shells and bombs in Afghanistan. They laid a roadside bomb but made such a mess of it, there was no explosion. The clean-up guys saw the disturbance in the road and were able to avoid the area and retrieve the bomb. While analyzing the cell phone traffic coming out of Lebanon they were alerted by another group but had not labeled them yet. They were planning an attack in the near future, but the specifics had not been determined yet.

Marko was glad to be back in an office and a daily

routine.   He felt comfortable in the Velgrove International Industries, NY office.   He assumed the helm as if he were born for it.   He rode his bicycle to work every day.   Connie assigned a bodyguard to Marko who complained about the bicycle at first but became accustomed to the ride and now even enjoyed it as much as Marko. He noticed on several mornings they seemed to be followed by some oriental looking riders but since it was not everyday he figured it was probably a riding club.

The riders were in direct contact with S.F. Lee in Shanghai.   After his all night at the casino, he got a report every morning before going to bed.   He had planned an accident.   In three days, they would push Marko into the path of an oncoming bus as they rode.

CHAPTER 24
TERRORISTS CHALLENGE

As Marko rode to work three days later, he felt his cell vibrating. He stopped at the corner and looked at the screen. He didn't recognize the number, but answered anyway.

"Hello, this had better be important."

"Mr. Fushier, I'm sorry to interrupt but we have a picture of a woman and we think its Mei-Ling Lee. I will send it to you now, please tell me if it is."

"Who is this?"

"Oh, I'm sorry. This is Cindy Bartell in Qatar."

"Thank you Cindy." Marko added, "Here is the picture now. Let me see. It looks really grainy but, yes that's Mei-Ling. Where is she?"

"We got this picture off a local camera in Baalbek in the middle of the Bakaa Valley just over the Lebanese Mountains directly west of Beirut. The family home of Ahmed Nahbi, someone in her chemistry class is there."

"Cindy, you are a smart woman. What do you think happened with Mei-Ling and this Ahmed?"

"From what we can tell so far, he brought her home with him from UCLA. The family has put her with the other women of the house. She doesn't talk to them because of language differences. I believe she may be able to speak French. They do not know this. We only know because there is a CIA contact working at the house. Ahmed beats her regularly just to prove his diligence to the family. She has tried to make him take her to an international phone, but the family watches them. He is careful to follow the family wishes, meaning the males of the family, you know. We are only able to listen to several cell phones and follow the emails. The CIA contact does the rest."

"Cindy, what goes on in that area?"

"If you mean the town, it is rural. There is irrigation and farming near the town. There is a fertilizer manufacturing plant there."

"Okay, okay. I guess what I'm asking is about military training or terrorism. I believe he took her to use her for a target. Do you have any indication of that in the messages you heard?"

"I don't listen, I only receive reports. Our Lebanese speaking researchers actually hear. I will need to call back with an answer for that question."

"Call me in an hour. I will be in my office by then."

She hung-up the phone and Marko continued riding his bicycle to work. He normally took East River Drive riding along the river to Madison. Today, instead of going along the river he headed straight to his office down Park Ave to Broadway arriving at the Broome Street office in only thirty minutes.

That change put the Asian bicyclers out of sync and

the attack never materialized. They arrived at the corner where Marko and the bodyguard should be passing and waited for twenty minutes. Marko never passed that way.

The office Marko inherited was very well appointed. There was a full living suite with bath, closet and bedroom. Long nights at work were never a hassle for the Velgrove brothers. Marko rushed to shower and dressed for his work day.

As he got to his desk his assistant, Rosalyn, lightly knocked and said, "Mr. Fushier, someone named Cindy has been calling. She is on line three."

Rosalyn had been promoted to Marko's assistant, since she was the only contact he had known within the personnel. He liked her persona. When he was a blackmailer, she handled it perfectly and when he was the boss, she segued into the right attitude. Nothing seemed to bother her.

"Thanks Rosalyn, don't put any calls through until I finish with Cindy. This is important."

"Sure, thing."

"Cindy, speak to me. This is Marko."

"We just made a break through," her voice sounded excited and hurried. "We got information about a proposed hit on a Northern European Country. The trouble is it just happened. The TV will be on it within the hour, maybe sooner. The man they arrested in Norway was a sitting duck who was called last night and sent to kill all the people in a youth camp. He later set off a bomb in Nobel Peace Prize Square."

"Where's Mei-Ling?"

"She's still in Lebanon. But we need to get her out. They're planning to move on Somalia. We haven't worked out exactly how it will go down, but they're either willing to murder hundreds of starving women and children or the UNESCO workers who are flying in to help. I'm sending an email with the report."

"Let me read it and I'll get back to you," Marko answered.

He started reading the email while considering his course of action.

To: *Marko Fushier*
From: *Cindy*
Marko this came from the local news.

> *The World Food Program (WFP) said Friday it will begin providing food for 175,000 people in the Gedo region of southwest Somalia and to 40,000 people in the Afgoye corridor northwest of the capital Mogadishu. Somalia's prolonged drought dissolved into famine because neither the Somali government nor many aid agencies can fully operate in areas of southern Somalia controlled by al-Shabab.*

> *The U.N. food agency also plans airlifts of aid to Mogadishu, WFP spokeswoman Emilia Casella told reporters in Geneva. On Wednesday, the U.N. declared a famine in the Bakool and Lower Shabele regions of southern Somalia, greatly raising the profile of what has*

been a steadily worsening food crisis in the Horn of Africa. The global body estimates that more than 11 million people in East Africa are affected by the drought, with 3.7 million in Somalia among the worst-hit because of ongoing civil war in the country. WFP's representative for Somalia warned Friday that the conditions for declaring a famine are expected to be reached soon in two further parts of southern Somalia — Juba and Bay.

The group in Lebanon has said they will attack the UN agencies providing food. They need to control the government in Somalia. The al-Shabab is closely controlled by al Qa'eda from Lebanon.

Marko turned on the television and watched the CNN station unfolding the Norwegian terrorist strike.

A square in Oslo, where the Nobel Peace Prize is awarded, was covered in twisted metal, shattered glass and documents expelled from surrounding buildings which housed government offices and the headquarters of Norway's leading newspapers. Most of the windows in the 20-floor high-rise where Prime Minister Jens Stoltenberg and his administration work were shattered simultaneously from the blast.

Marko picked up the phone, dialed Garland and dialed Connie on his cell phone. As he waited for them to come online he considered the options.

"Garland, Connie, I have an emergency. How well trained are the anti-terrorist corps? I want to move into Lebanon and Somalia immediately. I want only a couple of people to go to Lebanon with me. The corps will go to Somalia. The al-Shabab group is going to attack the famine workers there. We need to stop the attack."

"Woah, kid, that's a lot'a wants right off the bat," Garland exclaimed.

Connie added, "It's too fast off the starting block. Let me have some'a my friends in Israel go over to Lebanon."

"I have to go. If Mei-Ling sees me, she will come with me." Marko countered.

Connie yelled, "You want to go get Mei-Ling."

"Yes," Marko answered, "This is the only sure way to get her back."

"Hell fire! Kid you can't just do that. There are police forces all over this world who will stop you."

"Connie, please listen."

"Marko, make this call a conference call so we can hear each other," Garland said, "Just have your new assistant Rosalyn do it, she knows how."

They all hung up and Marko buzzed Rosalyn asked her to conference call the brothers. She asked, "Shall I include Chung and Farimo as well?"

Marko asked her not to include the older brothers since he probably would have trouble dealing with the two he had picked already. If he had all four on the phone they surely would override anything he wanted.

The phone buzzed and as Marko picked it up Garland said, "Okay kid, let's hear this again."

Marko explained about the emails from Qatar and the information found by the CIA. After explanations, the two brothers were more agreeable and started making plans to cooperate with Marko.

Connie would contact his Israeli people from Horizon Industries, who would find Mei-Ling and get her out of Lebanon. The Velgrove anti-terrorist corps would move into Somalia through Djibouti using its strategic geographic location at the mouth of the Red Sea where France maintains a significant military presence in the country, but Djibouti also has strong ties with the US. Hosting the only US military base in sub-Saharan Africa.

"You must not put yourself in danger," Garland added. "We have one young Velgrove in danger; please do not put yourself in jeopardy with her."

"I will not intentionally put myself or Mei-Ling in jeopardy, but I will get her back here safely." Marko continued, "I don't know if either of you have ever really been in love, but this is really it for me. I don't want to continue with this charade if she doesn't come back. I don't want to be part of something that doesn't care about people. So let's get her back here."

"Well, son, I guess we have our work cut out for us, don't we," Garland drawled in his old Texas cowhand way. "We'd better get to work, Connie. Who do you have to call in Israel?"

"That's easy. Aaron can go into Lebanon without being detected and he does Muslim almost as good as the real thing. Marko, I will make arrangements for you to meet with Aaron in Haifa tomorrow afternoon at the Hilton Hotel lunch counter. You should do your homework in the meantime and try to look like something other than a university professor."

"Thank's, Connie. Garland, how soon can the Velgrove corps go to Djibouti?"

"I have already notified them to prepare. I emailed them while we spoke."

"You guys are amazing," Marko exclaimed, "I'll be in contact after I'm on my way. This may be a problem to get reservations."

"Dude! What's wrong with the corporate jet? It's setting right there in New Jersey Airport waiting to be used," Connie answered.

"You guys keep me straight. I'm not accustomed to all the benefits,"

"I'll have the corps leaders, Laurie and Nonna give you a breakdown of what they have available," Garland added.

"There are two women in charge?"

"Laurie is a guy, you won't believe how tough he is," Garland answered.

"I can see right away, I have a lot to learn."

"Please, be careful, we cannot lose you, now that you have found us," Connie added.

"Laurie will also meet you in Haifa. I just heard from him. They've been briefed by the Qatar group.

He's sending Nonna to the Somalia fiasco. Soon we'll need to make ourselves known to the United Nations or some group with enough clout to cover our adventures into the wild, wild world," Garland continued. "We can get away with one of these excursions but don't think it will be easy to cover. Connie is better in cover-up than anyone alive, but even he is cringing over this one."

"I'll call Farimo. He may have some additional input, especially about Somalia. I have an answer from Aaron. He will be waiting for you; the plane is flying to LaGuardia. It'll make it easier for you. You need to stop talking and start moving." Connie ended the conversation, "Goodbye, kid."

Garland chimed in, "Go with the wind, son."

"Thanks," answered Marko.

Marko gave instructions to his assistant, rushed from the building with a bag packed hurriedly from his office closet. He caught the first cab available headed for LaGuardia. As he sat in the cab he started to meditate. He had been practicing these methods since the morning in Hong Kong when the Yoga Coach came to his hotel room and discussed the meditation and yoga practices of his teacher Maharishi Mahesh. Marko let the noise of the engine and the city blend with his brain waves making his head absolutely empty. He didn't have to hum or make any noises, he was in a small boat gliding down a river shaded by trees overhead as his mind reached higher and higher for more information. He had solved some problems while in the trance or whatever you wanted to call this. He didn't solve anything today. He was probably too preoccupied with his trip. Maybe he could continue meditating on the plane, if he didn't have interruptions. He couldn't get over the private jet thing. He kept thinking about sitting beside crying babies or snoring old guys.

Marko found the jet waiting at La Guardia and was taken to the boarding ramp by a special airport transport. He boarded and was immediately assured they would be taking off as soon as the pilot returned with the flight plans.

Marko relaxed. He thought, "Here we go kiddo. I'll find her and I'll never let her go again. She must have been really angry with me to have left with Ahmed Nahbi. I wonder what she thought she would accomplish. She is an educated woman, who can run her own life. She has a doctorate in chemistry. Dear God please let me find her alive."

-----o-----

S.F. Lee was angrier than Raymond had ever seen him. He ordered the Tai chi masters home to Shanghai immediately and fired them. They were sent back to their dojo in Xinjing. The planning started again. Raymond made sure the men were paid and had no idea of the mad actions of S.F. Lee.

He said to Raymond, "We will teach 'the idiot' a lesson."

"Let's see what he does, 'the idiot' may surprise you." Raymond answered.

"He disappeared. How could that happen?"

"The guys at the office, said he had gone to the middle east to bring back your sister."

"That idiot! He's putting himself in jeopardy over a woman?" S.F. Lee answered.

"Dude, it's your sister, don't you care?"

"No man. She never did a thing for me. Why should I care?"

"What are you going to do next?" Raymond asked.

"I'm not going to the middle east, that's for sure."

CHAPTER 25
MARKO FINDS MEI-LING

Aaron met Marko at Haifa airport. Everyone had been briefed except Marko. They continued on to Damascus, Syria. Aaron described every possible scenario they might encounter. He gave Marko all his information while the driver took them out Highway 1 leading to Beirut, Lebanon. The Qatar Group had established a good cover story for Marko. In today's Beirut Newspapers an announcement that the distant grandson of famous French economist, Francois Queenay who wrote 'Tableau Economiques' would be at the *Lebanese University*, Beirut – Lebanon's Rafic Hariri University to lecture on International Input-Output.

As the driver Arles headed into the countryside, Aaron explained, "We're headed to Baalbek, about seventy-five miles away. We've sent two operatives ahead to approach the house contact where Mei-Ling is being held. They will get her out of the house and it is our job to get her into our car and leave with her. It won't be easy. If that fails for some reason, like they can't get her out of the house or her escort becomes spooked or a hundred other reasons, we will proceed to the University where you will give your speech and we will go back to Damascus."

By midnight they reached Baalbek and went to a small house inside a fenced barricade. Marko was taken to a bedroom. He had not slept in 36 hours or more, flown half way across the world and had lost track of the days and the correct time. It was dark, it had to be night. He thought sleep would be impossible, but as his head hit the pillow he slept. Aaron woke him in the morning and they drove to the market near the Nahbi household. Marko wore a khaki suit with white open shirt. He and Aaron got out of the car and walked through the market area to the coffee stand where they sat and ordered. When the coffee arrived they took the cups and walked through the vegetable stalls. They bought a few bags of fruit and were walking to the other side when Marko saw two women in burqas walking in the market. He walked toward them, only their eyes were showing and they looked down. He was sure it would be Mei-Ling, but it wasn't.

Aaron leaned close and said, "We must go now. They would have been here by now, if they could get away."

Marko just shook his head, "Five more minutes, what could it hurt, we'll just drive a little faster."

So they walked around the market one more time. As they reached the car there were women walking toward the market from across the street. Marko strained his eyes to look, but could not see anyone who could be Mei-Ling. Aaron proceeded to the Range

Rover and got into the back seat, as Marko turned to sit, someone grabbed his hand. He looked at the eyes that met his directly. He jumped into the car pulling her in also and yelled to the driver, "Go, go, go!"

Marko wrapped his arms around her and said, "I'll never let you go again."

"I knew you would come. Don't ask me why. I just knew."

He began unwrapping her from the black robes. She was bruised everywhere. Aaron gently wrapped her back up and laid her on the floor of the car. Marko began to object, but Aaron explained, "We must drive forty miles before we cross the border into Syria. We won't be safe until then. We drive as inconspicuously as possible until we are safely in Damascus Airport."

Mei-Ling was shaking as she lay across their feet on the floor. Marko kept his hand on her shoulder. She finally stopped crying and lay still. She said, "Marko, please, please forgive me. I was such an idiot. They gave me that date rape drug the night after graduation. At first it felt good being 'out of it' then I came around and remembered part of what happened. By then they had me on a plane. They are going to bomb the Somalia refugee camp. These people are so jaded. They see no value in any person not of their own kind. You must intercept the Somalia bombing. Is there anyone we can tell and make it stop?"

Aaron responded, "Yeah, sure we're on it. We already have a unit going there. Tell me all you know so we can intercept the bombers."

"They were speaking in French. I didn't let them know I spoke French. I spoke a few words of Arabic and English. I heard about the Somalia bombing by chance. They said they would walk into the camp like refugees, go to the medical tent and detonate. They laughed that starving people and those 'infidels' would be killed."

"Okay, okay, talk more later. Here we go. Mei-Ling roll under the seat as much as possible. This is your first test. They haven't had time to know you are missing. Okay, here we go."

They slowed for the traffic check. The guard looked in the window and waved them past the blockade. They drove away carefully making sure not to hesitate or speed. They could not make phone calls on their cells, for fear of being intercepted. They had to trust the screen they initiated at the market had worked.

The woman accompanying Mei-Ling had been taken for questioning by the police. The CIA operatives had reported her as suspicious. The police had picked her up and were questioning her at the local station. They would let her go eventually. Only then would the Nahbi family know Mei-Ling was missing and they might not report it. The embarrassment to their family was more important than any woman.

As they left the barricade Marko's cell rang.

"Hello, this is Marko Fushier."

"Professor Fushier, this is Carman Hariri Professor of Macroeconomics, Lebanon University. We've sent an entourage to escort you from the Syrian border and they cannot find you. Your speech is scheduled in an hour and one-half."

"Professor Hariri, it is so very kind of you to send an escort. Let me check with the driver to see where we are. Shall I call you back? This may take a few minutes."

"If you would like."

"What are they saying?" Aaron demanded.

"She's providing an escort and they can't find us. The speech is in ninety minutes." Marko answered.

They discussed the situation and decided they had to have Marko go to the University as a cover. They would let the driver, Arles, escort Mei-Ling to the airport. Aaron would stay with Marko and they would have a flat tire when the escort arrived.

Marko made the call, "Professor Hariri, the driver made a wrong turn early this morning, we are twenty miles east of Rayak, we are entering Jdita now and proceeding east. I got a fantastic look at Lebanon's environmental resources and am tremendously impressed by the role you have played in this development. Oh dear! It seems we have a bad tire. If you have your people pick us up at Jdita truck stop my driver will be able to stay with the car and have the repairs made in time for our return to the Damascus Airport. Does that sound like a workable plan?"

"I believe I can contact the escort team. Oh yes, they are waiting at the other side of Jdita hoping to pick up your trail there."

"Thank you for your help with this," Marko replied

and hung up the phone.

"They are waiting for us? Arles, pull over there and ruin a tire, so we're not liars," Aaron added. "We will limp into the truck stop to make this real."

"What's going to happen? Who will protect Mei-Ling?"

"You are protecting Mei-Ling by giving this speech. She will have time to get to the airport. Arles, is a registered driver allowed to drive across the border for fares all the time."

Aaron continued, "Mei-Ling, you must stay hidden under the seat cushion here in the back. Arles will be watched. You must stay hidden! Do not move. Do not make noise. This is not over yet."

The Range Rover pulled behind a group of trees, Arles grabbed a large spike and stuck it into a back tire. He hammered with a rock until it was spewing air and broke it off. He jumped in the driver's seat and got back on the highway. As they turned the corner, the truck stop loomed ahead. Mei-Ling was under the seat. She had wrapped herself in the burqa and jumped under the seat without a question. Marko assumed his university professor persona. As they reached the truck stop the wheel began to bump and roll crooked. Marko and Aaron jumped out and moved toward the gas station office. Arles continued rolling toward the tire restoration area. He told the station assistant he needed a tire really fast because he would be late to the Airport for an important fare if he didn't hurry. He waved some money at the attendant who responded by putting the vehicle into the repair bay and started working.

In about five minutes an SUV pulled into the station and started looking around. Marko and Aaron stepped out the station's front door. An obvious bodyguard walked up to them and asked if one of them was Marko Fushier. Marko stepped forward and shook the man's hand.

"I am Professor Fushier. Are you from the university?"

"The man stepped back and took his hand away saying, "Yes, Madam Hariri, asked we take you to the University for the speech."

"Great! Let's get going I'm going to be late if we don't go fast. What is your name?"

"My name is Hyram."

They went to the SUV and entered the back seat with Hyram. The driver pulled out toward Beirut. They drove steadily for over an hour finally coming to the university and going directly to a building where they helped Marko and Aaron out of the van and escorted them into the auditorium. Professor Hariri greeted Marko as a colleague. They had met briefly at a New York conference three years ago.

He said, "Professor Hariri it's so nice to renew your acquaintance. Is there any subject you especially need me to cover?"

"Professor Fushier, I'm sure you will give your subject total coverage as always. I will introduce you in about five minutes."

"Thank you, could I freshen up? We've been

driving for hours," Marko added.

"Of course, Hyram, please assist Professor Fushier."

Hyram took Marko to a restroom and held the towel while he splashed his face with water. He allowed him to go into a stall alone, but otherwise stayed with Marko the whole time. Aaron stood in the hallway outside watching the others for any strange movements. He was satisfied they were still unsuspected of taking Mei-Ling. Marko came out and walked into the auditorium for the speech. Marko had not made a speech like this in over a year. He was a little nervous. He had the information, maybe he would just teach a class. He sat and did a two minute meditation, looked up as Professor Hariri motioned for him to stand.

He was amazed as he looked out at his audience seeing them for the first time and realized they looked like students everywhere. Here at Lebanese International University they were no different, with book bags and trying to take down every word in their notebooks.

"Thank you, Professor Hariri. This morning I was taken on a tour of your country around Hammana. Lebanon's free-market economy and a strong laissez-faire commercial tradition do not restrict foreign investment. Lebanese service-oriented economy's main growth sectors include banking and tourism. Political stability following the Doha Accord of May 2008 helped boost tourism and, together with a strong banking sector, enabled real GDP growth of 7% per year in 2009-10 despite a slowdown in the region.

Marko Fushier, Harvard Professor of Economics continued speaking for almost an hour, describing details of Input-Output Matrix, Flow of Funds fluctuations and indicators reviewing policies, viewpoints and effects on their economy.

Aaron was behind the stage with the bodyguards and driver from the car that picked them up at the station. They talked quietly and he was able to get a good indication of their purpose and their hirers. So far he was sure Marko was safe here, but they did need to leave soon.

The Range Rover was traveling steadily toward the Damascus Airport. As Arles drove out of the truck station, he was sure a pick-up was following him. He drove steadily toward the Syrian border. As he got close to the border the pick-up pulled away and turned off into a side road. Arles drew a breath and relaxed a little. He still had to go through the border check. Usually he never had a problem. He pulled up to his normal lane but there was a new employee.

The new deputy asked Arles to get out and show his papers to the guard in the booth. As Arles walked from the booth putting his papers away he looked as the new guy pulled out his gun and shot into the back seat.

"What the hell are you doing?" Arles yelled.

"Hey Buddy, what's the difference? You don't carry no bomb, do you?" The guard laughed, walked back to the booth and slammed the door.

Arles was petrified that he had shot Mei-ling. He had to be careful or more would follow this shooting.

Arles purposefully started the car and left the border area. He drove the speed limit. Finally he pulled into a roadside area went around to check the damage.

He opened the back door and got inside, lifted the seat and looked down at Mei-Ling. She looked okay, she wasn't moving. He asked, "Are you alright?"

"Aaah, not really," she answered. "He hit my leg. I can't feel much there."

"Are you bleeding?"

"Some, but you must drive on, right?"

"I can hear you if you talk, please say something if the bleeding gets worse," Arles pleaded with her.

He returned to the driver's seat and started driving. He heard some movement, got no answer when he talked to Mei-Ling. He got to the airport drove onto the tarmac and up to the plane. Someone inside the plane saw him, opened the door and put down the stairs. He grabbed Mei-Ling, threw her over his shoulder and carried her into the plane. He left her with the pilot and attendant, left the plane and drove out to the highway. He contacted the team and told them what had happened. A man named Ari had answered. He said, "Marko and Aaron will be picked up from the University. We will deliver them to the Beirut Airport. You will fly to Thessalonica where Connie and Chung wait with medical help."

Marko finished his speech. Aaron took him by the arm escorting him to an unfamiliar car and they left the university. They arrived at the Beirut airport went directly to the Qatar plane waiting there, boarded and flew away.

When they were safely on the plane Aaron told Marko what had happened.

Aaron added, "We're just happy everyone got out alive. Mei-Ling is the only one who was injured. Arles will come out now. I'm sure he's been identified."

Marko said, "Let's make sure he doesn't get lost in the shuffle. Get him out and bring him to the New York Office. We'll offer him a job in the Velgrove Anti-terrorist Group. We'll find a place for him and for you if you need it."

Aaron answered, "Thanks, taking him out of the country will help keep the operation under cover."

"Can you handle the arrangements or do I need to contact Connie for details on managing the transfer out of the country?"

"No, no, I can handle it," Aaron continued. "You need to know something, though. You're being followed by three Chinese guys from Shanghai."

"What! What does that mean?" asked Marko.

"We've been so busy just getting in and out of here, I haven't had time to analyze the data, but we'll have lots of time now."

"Do you suppose Chung asked some of his security people to accompany us?"

"That's one possibility. There are many others."

CHAPTER 26
LOVE MONEY AND WAR

Marko and Aaron landed at the Aerodromio Makedonia, Thessalonika, Greece quickly unloaded their bags and jumped into the waiting Range Rover. They proceeded along Thessalonikis-Neon Moudanion highway to Agia Triada where Connie's house was located. Positioned on Thessalonikis-Neon Moudanion, Mikra Highway running along the top of the cliffs circling the Thessalonikis Kolpus in a strategic observation point dominated by the view of Aegean Sea's southern approach to Turkish Straits.

Arriving at the Kaulas estate, they were astonished by the massive building construction going on at the estate next door.

When Connie received the message of Mei-Ling's injury, he swung into action. He bought his neighbor's house. The house had been empty for years. Connie called the owner and made an offer. He contacted his school-mate who worked at the local University Hospital. Greece was in dire need of medical facilities. He could get elaborate government perks with the gift of a hospital here. Equipment was being unloaded; fences and driveways were being changed. There were nurses, doctors and physical therapists walking back and forth, trying to set-up all the equipment being delivered.

Marko and Aaron walked toward Connie's seaside house. Marko saw a familiar face in the middle of all the equipment.

"Connie, where do we go?" Marko yelled.

Connie turned and motioned for them to walk toward him. He took Marko's arm and asked, "Don't you want to rest first? You've had a hell of a trip."

"No. Connie I need to see Mei-Ling. I must see her even if she's asleep. I need to know she's alright. What's been done for her? Don't we need to fly her to the United States? The best doctors are in Boston, you know. I can get her to the best."

"We had the doctors flown here. We have it covered. You have to trust us sometimes."

Aaron stood back and watched the discourse between uncle and nephew.

"Well, where is she?"

"Come on, I'll show you."

They started walking. Inside the front door, the house was already beginning to look like a small community hospital. First was an entrance office, where they were instructed to follow the hallway to the left. Through the open door at the end of the hallway, Marko saw Chung and Nila sitting beside a bed.

As they reached the room, Chung stood, walked out and closed the door.

"Marko, she's been calling your name. The doctor

put her into an induced coma. That seems to be the new treatment allowing patients to recover without human intervention. She's lost so much blood. But she's not in pain at this time."

"Chung, I must sit with her. I need to know she is okay."

"Marko, she is not okay. She will have a long recovery. Those people did more harm to that beautiful lady than we will ever know."

Marko began to cry, "Chung, I can't lose her. I've lost so much, my mother, my father, I can't lose her."

Connie stepped in and hugged Marko saying, "Kido, we're doing everything possible. She has the best treatment. We will win this."

"I appreciate all you've done. I see the activity. Can't I just sit with her for a few minutes?"

Connie continued, "Chung, can't you let him see her a little while?"

Chung answered, "Yes, of course. Nila needs to rest now; I'm only concerned that Marko know what the future may hold."

The door opened and Nila motioned for Marko to enter. She hugged him, took his hand guiding him to a chair beside the bed. She sat beside him. They both watched as Mei-Ling breathed and the tubes supplied nutrients and medicine. She had tubes in her nose for breathing, down her throat to keep the airway open, in her arm for blood and other necessary liquids.

Marko sat there with tears running freely down his face. He moved closer and took her hand in his. He held on and moved his chair forward laying his head on the bed next to her arm. Nila rose, stroked his hair and left the room.

There was so much work moving things around and supervising the construction, Connie and Aaron both helped complete the hospital. After three days, the hospital was running smoothly, even treating local patients as well. Chung and Nila kept close watch on their daughter and Marko.

Marko spent most days talking to her and slept every night in Mei-Ling's room, mostly sitting with his head next to her arm and shoulder. He had watched while the leg bandage was changed. The bullet had shattered the leg bone causing immense damage to the veins and arteries. There was no circulation in the lower leg. The leg became more infected each day. After the fourth day, Mei-Ling's doctor announced, "We must remove the lower leg or she will die. The antibiotics are the best, but she had too much injury inside and out."

Marko asked, "What do you mean?"

The doctor answered after getting permission from Chung. "Mr. Fushier, she has internal injuries of the rectum and vagina, three broken ribs one of which punctured the right lung, a concussion and that doesn't include the leg. The leg has gangrene, broken bones and no circulation."

"Oh God, what did they do to her?"

"She was raped multiple times then had a piece of metal stuffed up there. We fixed the inside as good as possible, but she doesn't have a uterus anymore. I believe if we remove the leg, it will give her a chance to recover. She will still be strong enough to fight the multiple infections," The doctor answered.

"By all means take off the leg. Do whatever you need to save her life. Her Father and Mother must give their approval, but I'm sure they will want this also," Marko declared.

"Her father and mother have signed the approval, but they asked me to speak with you about their daughter," the doctor said.

Marko walked back into the room and started talking to Mei-Ling, "My darling, wife to be, the doctor plans to remove that lower leg hurting you so much. We'll just get rid of it. You'll feel much better without it. I promise you the most beautiful leg in the whole world. We will go leg shopping. We'll find the best one for you. You can live without a leg. I cannot live without you."

A nurse came into the room and said, "Mr. Fushier, I'm sorry, but we have to prep Miss Lee for the surgery. Please wait outside. We will be going to the surgery suite in about ten minutes."

Marko went to the room in the other house which had been assigned to him for sleeping and working. He immediately logged on to the internet and searched for amputated limbs replacement. He spent two hours searching and printing the information. He went back to the hospital building and sat outside the operating room. After three more hours the doctor came out and sat with the family.

He said, "Well, I believe we've made the difference. We'll watch for the next twenty-four hours. If she does well I suppose the worst will be over."

The family all talked at once.

"Thank you Doctor, we are so grateful."

"Thanks Doc."

"Doc, that's great!"

"When can I see her?"

The doctor stood, waved his arms and shook his head, saying, "The medical team is doing the best job possible. They're all responsible. She'll be in a drug induced coma for twenty-four hours then we'll start the process, letting her become cognitive of her surroundings. She's been through a traumatic experience and will need at least a year to recover and probably more like three before she is comfortable in her own skin. We're planning a recovery process that can be done here or in Boston or New York, where do you think we should set-up the next portion of the process?"

Marko stepped into the circle, "Doctor, what is your name, I didn't catch it?"

"My name is Mosley, Kenneth Mosley."

"Thanks Dr. Mosley. Don't you think it's too early to make plans for Mei-Ling? When she's better she can make her own plans. She's in this predicament, because someone made decisions for her. We're not going to make the same mistakes."

"Yes, yes, of course, sir."

Chung took Marko's hand, "Thank you, son."

Nila said, "I'll be in the room down the hall."

Connie stepped forward, "Doc, how long before she's cognitive?"

"She'll be sedated for four to five days yet, but in twenty-four hours we'll let her begin to be knowledgeable of her surroundings."

"We need to talk, Chung, Marko. Please meet me in the other house about five. I have some information we must go through." Connie walked down the hall toward the exit door.

Chung and Marko went to Mei-Ling's room where Nila watched the nurses bring her back from surgery. Finally Chung turned to Marko and said, "There is nothing we can do here. Come with me. We will go have some tea and talk."

"I'd rather stay with Mei-Ling but I'll come back later. I'll be here all night. I must be with her when she wakens."

"She may not like the first person she sees," her father said.

"I'll take that chance."

They went to the hospital kitchen, where a cook was making cinnamon buns. The aroma was heavenly. He heated the water for their tea and served it at the table on the porch overlooking the Aegean Sea. They watched as the ocean liners and tankers made their way to docks in Thessalonikis or as they came around the point from Alexandropoulos. This was a calming view and for almost thirty minutes the two sat there without speaking. All thoughts were questioning and planning and finally they looked at each other. Chung spoke first,

"Marko, you must not blame yourself. She did make her own decisions."

Marko replied, "Chung, she did not make any decisions to go there. They took her. They mutilated her. That little punk will pay."

"He will pay all his life. He knows what he did and he will never be able to walk down a street without looking behind to see who's following him," Chung added.

"He thinks he got away with it at this point." Marko continued, "He won't expect the coverage in Somalia."

"Connie probably has some information about that. I suspect he's been actively seeking more information while we've been preoccupied with Mei-Ling. It's time for me to go home where I can control my businesses better."

Marko spoke, "Chung I will be here until Mei-Ling is able to leave with me. I will not abandon her again. I did that once, I won't do it again. I would like your approval of our relationship, but I will not give up on it if you refuse to approve."

"Marko, I will give you my approval when Mei-Ling does."

"Thank you Chung, that's fair."

"We should go see what Connie has up his sleeve."

The too men, one Chinese over eighty years old, the other a thirty year old tall slender curly haired Harvard Professor walked to the house across the driveway and down the street. The beautiful Greek hills one side and the idyllic ocean on the other was diametrically opposed to their emotions. The two men walked toward Connie's estate.

Connie met them at the door with his young son who was walking now. His wife, Amanda, was in the living room where they sat and tried to be pleasant in the presence of Amanda and Shimmy. They talked about the boat they had seen while walking over and the weather. Connie eventually said, "Well, fellows lets go into my study. Please excuse us, Amanda. We need to talk business."

"I understand, Connie."

"Da, Da, wan to see." Shimon tried to talk.

Connie took Shimon's offered hand, "Shimmy, buddy, let mommy take you to the playground. Okay, buddy?"

The three men continued on to the study before speaking. Chung said, "What a great boy you have, Connie."

"Yes, I'm finding it to be a problem not having him around."

Marko spoke, "That's good, right?"

"I always said I would raise my own children. I always felt like a step child. Of course, I was a stepson, right Chung?"

Chung knew Connie had dealt with his birth-right long ago. They sat in the room looking out over the water. Connie started the conversation.

"We've more information about the Ahmed Nahbi family. They're working with the al Qa'eda central leadership. Planning attacks against any place that will make high impact on the world news. I want to be as clear as I can about the danger we face." Connie stopped and looked at both his brother and nephew before continuing.

"This is a form of warfare. We are standing watch on this threat, and we have produced our expeditionary force to actually help capture or kill those behind the threat. We are mostly fighting an intelligence campaign but with the most dangerous terrorists. We have conducted lawfully, responsibly, with a clear and single purpose of getting terrorists off the street and gaining intelligence on those still at large. People cannot fly overseas without fear. We must follow through on this project. Yes, it's a project and as long as we treat it like that we will handle it appropriately and legally."

Marko asked, "What additional information has been found while we were occupied? What is Ahmed up to?"

"Forget Ahmed, let me continue," Connie declared. "It's a highly complex struggle, a long term struggle and it's fought on two levels. The *Close Fight* is what we'll be doing with the Velgrove Corps. It's about people who want to kill, they can't be stopped unless we kill or capture them. There is the *Deep Fight*. It requires discrediting and eliminating the jihadists' ideology which motivates their hatred and violence. It requires winning what is essentially a war of ideas. Some of the actions required by the *Close Fight* can make fighting the *Deep Fight* even more complicated. Dealing with the immediate threat must naturally be a top priority.

Killing or capturing terrorists keeps them at bay and protects people, but defeating the world view responsible for producing those terrorists diminishes the threat itself. Winning the war of ideas actually defines the long term victory we seek. The war of ideas is not about the religion of Islam, it's about fanatics whose victims have usually been other Muslims. Terrorists must be exposed for the scourge they are, reviled for the horror and suffering they inflict. Only then can they be exposed at their source. The *Deep Fight* is a fight our whole society must wage. The *Deep Fight* requires jihadists' ideas of violence, extremism and intolerance be countered by ideas of peace, moderation and inclusion. It requires a tireless global campaign by a broad coalition of nations and societies. But frankly, it's our friends in the Islamic world, repulsed by al Qa'eda's savage distortion of their faith, who must take a leading role. In the global media al Qa'eda can attempt to spread its grand illusion or it can be where its operatives are revealed as murderers who try to justify their atrocities with a violent bankrupt ideology."

Chung asked, "Connie, what action do you have in mind?"

"As you know my expertise is media. In the long run that is the way we win this battle. I am calling a family meeting, or better said, I'm asking you, Chung, to call a family meeting. We are all in the midst of multiple crises at the moment but in six months we should all be able to meet in Brazil without causing too much disruption. By then Mei-Ling should be able to travel."

Chung asked, "By then you will be able to formulate a media campaign, right?"

"I'll do my best." Connie replied. "I know you must return to Hong Kong soon."

"What about the Velgrove Corps?" Marko asked.

"Don't worry we're keeping that in the mix."

Marko continued, "I'm going to have my plate full trying to manage Velgrove, NY. Could someone else take over the Corps?"

"We will discuss all of these possible scenarios when we have the family meeting." Connie replied.

Suddenly Chung made a strange noise. Connie and Marko looked at him. He was staring out the window where Nila had set-up an easel and was painting the scene over the trees where the Aegean and the Greek Isles were.

Chung shook his head, "She relaxes when she paints. She must be so terribly upset by all this. She blames me for sending Mei-Ling to UCLA in the first place."

Connie concluded, "Chung that was before the kidnapping. She can't blame you. We need to pay for this hospital. All these doctors and equipment cost a lot. If we each throw in we can do it without hurting any of the businesses. It works the same as with the Corps. We already covered that. This hospital can be converted into a training facility if we connect with The Aristotle University of Thessaloniki. It is the largest university in Greece and the Balkans. Its campus covers 230,000 square meters in the centre of the city of Thessaloniki.

They already have some educational and administrative facilities located off campus for practical and operational reasons. They have a Special Technical Laboratory Staff for teaching services and members of administrative staff. The AUT performs research in a variety of scientific fields. It's constantly in close cooperation with universities, organizations and research centers both in Greece and abroad. The large number of faculties and approximately 250 laboratories enable scientists of the AUT to carry out this variety of research projects. During the past 12 years, 4500 research programs were undertaken and realized with the participation of more than 10,000 members of the academic community and several external collaborators. That Research Committee has a member who went to school with me in England. He will be glad to take charge of the Velgrove Hospital and supervise research here. It's even possible it will convert to a money maker. But that can be talked about at the family meeting."

Chung stood and said, "We should be getting back to the hospital, Marko. Connie, Nila and I will leave tomorrow. Until then I must be with my daughter. Please contact me by phone."

Chung and Marko walked from the house over the recently constructed driveway to the hospital. Mei-Ling looked angelic asleep in her bed. They both stood staring at the love of their lives. Finally, Marko sat and laid his head next to her arm as he had before.

Chung spoke, "I'm leaving Mei-Ling in your care. I know you will take care and see she gets what she needs. I will leave soon. You will have to explain why we amputated her leg."

Marko sat up and said, "Oh, Chung, her leg is so unnecessary if she is alive and with us. Don't beat yourself up about that, please."

They both sat, one on either side of the bed. When Marko awoke, Chung was gone. Marko started talking to Mei-Ling.

"I want to tell you about my mother, because you remind me of her. My mother knew more about me than any other person. She was unusual in her demeanor. She was this petite, bright red haired woman who loved every person she ever saw. When I was a child, she took me along as she shopped and did her work. One day we went to the pet hospital. I didn't know why. We went to the Animal Shelter. She showed me how the animals were treated there. And then she asked me if I wanted to help out after school. Every day I went to the 'dog pound' and before long I had kept twenty dogs from the euthanizer. I found homes in my neighborhood, among my friends at school and people I met on the street. My mother had an unexplainable ability to become instant friends with even brief acquaintances. People looked at her and she exuded trust. People she met in the market confided the most amazing details, experiences or troubles. Many times she returned from shopping trips telling about the store people who waited on her, the shoe clerk whose wife was about to undergo open heart surgery, or the dress maker whose son was in trouble with the law. She didn't just listen to their troubles, she tried to help them. She told them of the best services in their field of need. She got a second opinion for the shoe clerk's wife saving many years of heart valve difficulties. She spoke to the consulate about the dressmaker's son and he was able to take a job in Peru continuing his education without going to jail. She carried the same abilities of instant trust into her husband's job as ambassador. He wasn't the ambassador, they were both the ambassador. Over the years she was able to assist her husband more than even he would admit. When he needed information he just let his wife know. On her next opportunity she listened to the other ambassador's wives, workers, servants, salespeople, soldiers, policemen -- there was no need for the diplomatic bartering. I'll tell you one, if you tell me one. She was just a lady gossiping, listening to the problems or complaints, checking with her friends, buying the daily necessities. Where her husband ran into a wall of silence, she found people only too willing to tell everything."

Marko talked until he no longer had any more stories. He told of his mother, his father's ambassadorial stories and his own university adventures. After a few hours Marko realized she was listening to him and then she made a sound. He called the nurse and asked if they might remove the tin thing from Mei-Ling's mouth. The doctor came to the room and checked her reflexes. He finally removed the breathing tube from her throat. The nurse gave her gargles and water to help take away the uncovered soreness. The doctor carefully explained about the amputation and many of her other injuries. She just listened. After the doctor left Marko sat by the bed and laid his head next to hers. He continued to talk and realized after awhile she was asleep again. Marko had told all his stories and was silent again.

CHAPTER 27
FAMILY COUNSEL – BRAZIL

Rurrenabaque a small colorful Amazonian town on the far eastern Andes spur sat between the north's Pampas del Yacuma savannahs where wildlife abounds, and south up the Beni River where Pilon Lajas Biosphere Reserve and Madidi National Park are.

Connie, Amanda and Shimon met Garland and Phyllis at the Rurrenabaque Airport. They had flown there on separate airlines.

The daughters of Garland and Phyllis were working and weren't coming. They took very little interest in the Velgrove businesses. They had their own careers in the travel industry. S.F. Lee would not be there and Farimo's sons were staying home to run the Cairo businesses.

The region with the greatest biodiversity in the world is in northwest Bolivian Amazon. Located in the transition zone between Amazon rainforest west of the Rio Beni and Amazonian "pampas" east of the Rio Beni, the ecosystems are protected in three reserves, Madidi National Park, Pilon Lajas Biosphere Reserve and Indigenous Territory, and the Pampas Reserve. The region forms part of the international corridor of protected areas extending from Vilcabamba in Peru to Amboro in Bolivia.

Several hours by 4WDrive on bumpy roads to the Yacuma River, or by dugout canoe up the Beni and Quiquibey or Tuichi rivers is always an adventure. The scenery varies and wildlife viewing opportunities are different but always spectacular. The Velgrove and Kaulas families traveled through the countryside talking about all the recent happenings.

Soon Garland started showing them why he had invested here. An Amazonian town, Rurrenabaque is a tropical experience. Exploring some of the best nature and wildlife hotspots in Bolivia combined with breathtaking landscapes; contribute to the popularity of tourism with jungle lodges and campsites deep in the savannahs of Pampas del Yacuma or the Chalalán rainforest at Madidi National Park. These locations serve adventurous travelers and photographers who are prepared for hot, humid and sometimes rainy weather. Local residents gain jobs and businesses from the tourism and biosphere reserves.

The lands adjacent to the park's eastern border are home to a large colonist population, occupying approximately 200,000 hectare along the Yacuma-Rurrenabaque road. These communities impart considerable pressure on the protected area's resources. Most settlers originated from the altiplano and arrived in one of two migration waves: the first occurred between 1978 and 1980 when the Yacuma-Rurrenabaque road was built, and the second wave occurred between 1983 and 1987 as a consequence of both an intense drought in the Department of Potosi and the closure of the State mines. It had taken Garland some time to realize that in Brazil all the states were called departments and were located in the State of Brazil.

In 1980 when Garland was twenty-five years old and just beginning to take over the companies from Vernon he became fascinated with the Bolivian reserves and the drive to preserve their ecosystem. Garland invested in the biospheres and when that turned into tourism he was glad he had. I Ie established various trip possibilities, from group tours to independent high risk, into the wild trips. Phyllis was his biggest supporter of the Bolivian investments. She had set up a wide spread tourist agency in Texas, expanded nationwide and eventually worldwide. Their two daughters also worked in the tourism industry.

The Mapajo Ecotourism Lodge project began in 1998 with support from the embassies of the United Kingdom and Canada, the Regional Amazonian Indigenous People Support Program (PRAIA), and the United Nation's Development Program. The investment totaled US$ 200,000, compared to the US$ 1.5 million investment in Chalalán in Madidi Integrated Natural Management Area. Mapajo changed its status from project to small community business when it started operating two years ago under its new name: Mapajo Ecoturismo Indígena S.R.L., paying rent to the communities for use of the infrastructure.

Garland said, "I'm gonna brag a little. This year, approximately 200 tourists arrived, traveling from Rurrenabaque on the Beni River. Conservation International helps promote the lodge and PRAIA provides a technician. A product of joint efforts between Asunción de Quiquibey and five surrounding communities, the emphasis differs from Madidi's Chalalán Ecolodge in that it focuses more on the area's cultural values. Its infrastructures reflect and respect traditional styles and the community operates a crafts center. The fact that this project has not yet benefited all communities has created several skeptics among the partners who hoped for quick results. Some of them started their own lodges independent of Mapajo, while others decided to abandon their tourist offering because of the problems encountered in the distribution of incomes."

Connie had to have input, "You must have had some difficulty with the local governments when you first started."

Garland continued, "I invested in the land surrounding the area. On the northern border of Bolivia, the Brazilian town of Rio Branco in Amazonas is at the beginning of the river which turns and twirls through the countryside. I saw a map of the area before buying. I thought the river looked like a rope coming unrolled, twisting and turning. I bought as much property as the government would sell a foreigner. I also loaned money to three Brazilian natives for making land investments. High in the hills about one thousand miles below the equator I manage more land than all the other brothers in all their companies throughout the conglomerate. In the area south of my land the biosphere reserve was established."

"Did you know beforehand that would happen?" Connie asked.

"It was planned. I knew the land would be worth the investment, but it was a stab in the dark. Establishing a biosphere reserve obviously posed an enormous challenge, namely to set up an appropriate mechanism, for instance a steering committee, to plan and co-ordinate all the activities taking place there. The human dimension of biosphere reserves made them special, since the management essentially became a "pact" between the local community and society as a whole. Management of a biosphere reserve needed to be open, evolving and adaptive. Such an approach required perseverance, patience and imagination. But it allowed the local community to respond to external political, economic and social pressures, which affected the ecological and cultural values of the area."

"The locals aren't always willing to cooperate with outsiders coming in to make decisions about their lives. What did you do about that?" Connie asked.

"The Biosphere Reserves are important ecosystems internationally recognized by UNESCO, where communities combine conservation of biodiversity with sustainable development. They are dominated by communities within a shared landscape to demonstrate how people can live and work in better harmony with nature. I helped my neighbors cope with the controls demanded by the Biosphere Reserves. I showed them that I was under the same controls and was able to make a profit with the demands established by the Bio People," Garland proceeded. "Here we are now. I always love coming back, like I'm going home. I call it my Garden."

Connie teased, "You mean Garland Garden?"

This Velgrove family meeting on Garland's property north of Rio Branco was scheduled for two business days followed by three leisure days and one more business day at the end. Chung and Nila had arrived first, choosing to travel by river boat to the Estate. They brought the load of food and supplies needed for the meeting.

On a trip back to Thessalonikis, Connie and Chung had talked, making plans and questioning their presently used processes. Garland and Farimo had met in Cairo several months ago and discussed the same problems. They all agreed businesses known to be owned by the family needed to change their investments and become extraneous. Chung called the meeting after Connie's request, but they all waited for Mei-Ling to become well enough for travel and making future decisions. Marko and Mei-Ling arrived together in Rurrenabaque Airport. A helicopter took them to the Estate revealing the area's terrain as they went.

The family was comfortably ensconced in their rooms. They each had a separate cottage with every convenience. They all gathered at 5:00pm for drinks, then dinner. Afterward Nila, Phyllis, Amanda, Adella and her three daughters, Simone, Petra and Nona, walked in the gardens behind the house. The garden had many rare plants and was the pride and joy of the gardener, Joseph, who took care to keep the specimens growing and happy. The orchid filled garden contained as many varieties as possible. Some were extinct except for this location.

Garland had taken it upon himself to consider his land part of the buffer zone and transition area around the Biosphere reserve zone. The legally established core area had given long-term protection to the landscapes, ecosystems and species it contained. As nature is rarely uniform and historical land-use constraints exist in many parts of the world, there may be several core areas in a single biosphere reserve to ensure a representative coverage of an ecological systems mosaic. Normally, the core area is not subject to human activity, except research, monitoring and traditional extractive uses by local communities. To learn about traditional forms of land-use, people in many parts of the world have devised ingenious land-use practices which do not deplete the natural resources and provide valuable knowledge for modern production systems. Biosphere reserves are areas where such peoples maintain their traditions, improving their economic well-being through the use of culturally, environmentally appropriate technologies.

A major obstacle to reconciling environment with development is the division of our opinions. Biosphere reserves provide places where conflicts of interest can be debated by all the stakeholders concerned, local officials, landowners, nature conservation associations, government leaders, scientists, local farmers, fishermen, private enterprises – all must work together to find appropriate co-ordination mechanisms to plan and manage the biosphere reserve. Biosphere reserves therefore provide opportunities for open discussion, information sharing and conflict resolution which could be applied in other development issues. Garland had always adhered to the information and results obtained in the reserves. That promotion alone was demonstration enough to local people that the biospheres worked in reality as well as theoretically.

Within this beautiful surrounding eco-center the meeting was about to begin. All the men met in the library waiting for Connie to explain his ideas.

"My friend Michael, who was with the CIA once, ran into us back in Greece. We had a chat. He was about to report to the Senate Intel Committee on counterterrorism. He said, 'waging a global, high stakes war against al-Qa'ida and other terrorists that threaten the United States remains a fundamental part of CIA's mission'. We work on our own, with other US Government agencies and with foreign liaison partners to target terrorist leaders and cells, disrupt their plots, sever their financial and logistical links and toss their safe havens."

Garland asked, "Where do they coordinate all this?"

"The CIA's war on terror is run from the Counter-

Terrorism Center and carried out from stations and bases overseas. CTC has both operational and analytical components. Fusion of these two is the key to success."

Marko broke in, "We work closely with the National Counter-Terrorism Center. Our collection of terrorist targets has been steadily improving in both quantity and quality."

"I guess they're running many local informants. Michael says access to information is a primary factor in an informant's value to them. Penetrating secretive terrorist organizations is among his greatest challenges. He made significant improvements though his greatest concern is damage done by leaks in recent years. Terrorist plots and groups are not broken by single reports or sources and no detainee knows everything about the compartmented activities of a group. Painstaking all-source analysis is crucial to supporting and driving operations. The work of CTC has been crucial to identifying and targeting terrorists, vetting assets and supporting overseas work."

Connie sat down after relating his discussion with the previous CIA director. The four brothers and Marko were listening in the library with their after dinner drinks. Mei-Ling opened the door and elegantly walked to the nearest chair and sat. They all just stared. They knew her left leg was amputated above the knee. She was wearing a prosthesis that ended in a spring foot. She could only walk short distances, but expected to get better. Marko asked, "Darling, may I fix you a drink?"

She shook her head. She was looking down, but

eventually looked each of the brothers in the eye before saying, "I am mad as hell. I am mad at each of you. I am mad at myself more than all of you put together. I will walk better soon. I may take over my father's Hong Kong company one day. I will teach Chemistry at NYU next year. You, Connie, do not rest until you find Ahmed Nahbi. That son of a bitch is going to die. One way or the other, he is going to die."

Garland spoke up, "Darling, he will have to live with his sins."

"Hell fire and damnation, Garland. I want him dead. He stuck a wire brush up my vagina and told me it was a bomb and if I removed it I would explode. He beat me every day in front of his family. Now you tell me he does not deserve to die a thousand deaths."

"My dear, dear niece I cannot imagine how much you have suffered, but the brothers are planning to take care of this as quickly as possible. Please don't suffer more over this no good hooligan."

"My only request is I see him dead and severed into pieces so he may not go to his heaven."

She stood and started to the door. "Don't think I'm not grateful for all you did. Thank you, Connie for treating me as a daughter. Thank you all for investing in the antiterrorist group and the hospital."

As the door closed, Farimo stood and started talking, "I don't usually speak first, but she is right. We must kill this dreg and quickly. She needs it, Marko needs it and the world needs it."

"Thank you Farimo," Marko said. "Yes, this matter

needs to be settled. He has even had the gall to contact her by email. I cannot be rational about the situation. I have asked Laurie and Nonna to concentrate on finding some place we can get at this... Oh I can't even say his name."

Chung cleared his throat and wiped his face. "I and Connie and Marko have collaborated with the Qatar Group on information. I do not want her to kill him. It will be so bad for her for a long, long time and I can't stand to see her hurt more."

"Yes I know what you mean." Connie added. "We have not found the scum yet, but I will. Between Farimo and me he will not have any wiggle room. It's only a matter of time before he surfaces someplace. When he does, Laurie and Nonna will be on him."

Farimo spoke up, "Laurie is that big guy with the red hair, right?"

Marko answered, "That's him. He is the calmest guy I've ever seen. He has nerves of steel."

Connie said, "If anyone can find the scum, Laurie will. We need to discuss plans for the companies to be known or public and we need to discuss the coordination of the less fortunate countries we reside in with our companies. Defeating the world view responsible for producing the jihadist ideology that motivates hatred and violence of terrorists diminishes the threat itself. I have outlined a media blitz campaign. Winning the war of ideas is the long term victory."

Farimo added, "The war of ideas is not about religion it's about fanatics and their victims. Terrorists must be exposed for the scourge they are, reviled for the horror and suffering they inflict. Only then can they be exposed."

Connie continued, "The *Deep Fight* is a fight our whole society must wage. The Deep Fight requires we countered jihadists' ideas of violence and extremism and intolerance by ideas of peace, moderation and inclusion. It requires a tireless global campaign. I believe we have connections in enough countries to make a dent in the ideas."

"You're right Connie," Farimo excitedly spoke, "it's our friends in the Islamic world, repulsed by al Qa'ida's savage distortion of their faith who must take a leading role. In the global media is where al Qa'ida can attempt to spread its grand illusion or its operatives can be revealed as murderers trying to justify their atrocities with a violent bankrupt ideology?"

"Here is the media strategy outline, please read it and tomorrow we will talk again," Connie said as he handed each a booklet.

Marko and Chung remained in the library after the others left the discussion. After a few minutes, Chung asked, "Marko, how is she, really?"

"Chung we have all learned so much in the last few months. Only recently has she been able to tell me what happened to her. She is so injured. She cannot trust anyone. What she said tonight is how she feels. I have encouraged her to just blurt out anything she remembers, because her senses were numbed, she could not feel at all for a long time. Now she is better in all ways. The leg doesn't seem to mean as much to her as to us. She wants to teach this fall and I think she should. She is becoming stronger everyday. And, yes, I still love her with all my heart. I should never have let her go away from me in the first place, but I could not manage all the changes in my life at that time so I let her go. She understands, possibly. Do you hear from her?"

"No she has not called us since her injury."

"Maybe this visit will make it easier for her to talk to you and Nila."

"We should go now. Have you seen this outline before?"

"I did see some of it, since the Input-Output Group and Qatar Group both worked on preparations."

"Well, goodnight Marko."

Marko walked through the garden with all its rare plants. Many orchids that could not be exported to other countries due to the laws enacted supposedly to protect the endangered species. He thought about how the good intentions had backfired making some plants extinct due to deforestation and not taking samples to be used in another location. Which made the most sense? What would make sense when the brothers talked tomorrow? He heard a movement in the bushes. When Marko looked into the dark he saw eyes staring back at him. A cougar crouched in the midst of the garden. Marko was in the kill zone of the great cat. The cougar could have taken him out. But he sat watching and planning. As Marko watched the large cat stood, stretched and majestically walked away into the night.

This was the most eerie feeling. Marko thought, "I was being watched, I had no idea of the danger and I walked right into his area. I was the stupid one; he knew exactly what was happening."

Marko went back to their room and slide into bed beside Mei-Ling. She turned to him and said, "I thought you would never get back."

"I just saw a cougar. It was the most eerie thing I've ever witnessed. I was walking through the garden when I realized something was watching me. I turned and there were the biggest eyes staring at me. It was as if he said hello then turned and walked away."

"Wow, darling, how could you not run?"

"Oh it was astounding. I think he told me something. As I meditate tomorrow, it will be revealed, I'm sure."

"You really like meditating, don't you? Maybe I should try it," said Mei-Ling.

"It can't hurt you. It may help you. It cleans the brainwaves and allows me to determine the most important answers to my questions. If I had learned it sooner I would never have let you out of my sight in the first place."

"Well how about this?" She moved on top of him, "Can this cat have a piece of you?"

He laughed and she tickled him before starting to kiss him all over. She had learned new ways to use her shortened leg to her advantage. He couldn't imagine her any other way.

The next morning, Marko arose at 5:00am as usual

and took thirty minutes' meditation to start his day. As he finished a thought came into his brain, "We can get Ahmed Nahbi by waiting. He will come out of hiding soon. We must be ready. Especially Mei-Ling must be ready. He had been so blatant in his emails to her and he will be overt in trying to get to her again. I must be the cougar in the dark waiting for him to strike. My time will come. Doug Henry would understand, if only I could reach him."

Mei-Ling was ready to go when Marko finished his shower and came into the room wrapped in a towel. She arose on her spring foot and walked to him and grabbed his private parts saying, "Pay attention. You have been preoccupied for an hour. What are you thinking about?"

"I think I would like to take you to meet a friend of mine in Peru when we finish here."

"That's nice. Maybe we could go tomorrow, during our three vacation days Connie has so generously given all of us."

"Would you do that? It might be a trek."

"Don't baby me! I told you before, don't baby me, ever."

She turned away from him and stomped out of the room. He quickly dressed and picked up his cell phone. When he left Doug in his isolated lodge, Marko left a satellite phone with Nissa. She answered on the third ring, "Hello Mr. Marko."

"Hello, Nissa, how is Doug?"

"Mr. Doug, he is okay. But Romero is very ill and

we must take him to the hospital in Sucre. We are leaving now. We should be there in three days."

"What is wrong?"

"He broke a rib but now he isn't breathing very well. Mr. Doug thinks a lung is stuck."

"Nissa, if you stay at the lodge, I will fly a helicopter there in about three to four hours and pick you up with Romero and Doug and we will take him to a hospital in Rio Branco. Ask Doug to wait. I will call back in thirty minutes with more information."

"Thank you Mr. Marko, I don't know how you do this?"

"I am in Rurrenabaque with my family."

Marko found Connie and Garland in the dining room having breakfast. "Hey, guys, I need to use the helicopter for about four hours."

They looked at him as if he were daft. Then recognized the Vernon Velgrove look that said, *Get out of my way, I'm coming through like it or not.*

Garland spoke first, "What's going on?"

Connie always had to get his word in, "That's sudden, isn't it. What about our conference?"

"I'll be back by mid-afternoon. I'll bring Doug Henry with me. He's an ex-treasury agent. I've wanted to get him involved with this from the beginning."

"He's the one who looked for Eileen, right?" Garland asked.

"That's the one."

Garland stood and said, "I'm assuming there is more to this than picking up Doug Henry. Maybe I should go too, you may need help."

It still amazed Marko the attitude of these brothers. Get on it. Let's go. Get it done. They could accomplish anything.

Marko thought for a minute, "Doug has a helper, Romero, who probably has a punctured lung and needs to be transported to the hospital. They would take three days to get him there. I said I would be there in a couple of hours. He's about a hundred miles above Sucre. That's closer to where we are. I said he should go to Rio Branco Hospital. I would like Mei-Ling to go with me."

"Get her and come to the garage. We need to get going," Garland answered.

Mei-Ling was glad to have a break from her mother. Nila couldn't let go of the leg tragedy. It was nice up to a point, seeing her mother again and feeling the love and care Nila exuded. The 'but' occurred when Mei-Ling wanted to continue with her life as if nothing were wrong with her. Mother just didn't understand. Her daughter should be pampered. As Mei-Ling started walking towards the garage with Marko, she laughed, "You may look like grandfather, but I've got just as much DNA, you can't see."

"Yeah, I know," Marko answered. "But you have to admit, we fit together pretty good, no?"

"You bet, dude."

She still amazed him with that 'hip' campus talk.

Garland loved to fly. So many times he had flown with other pilots who got into trouble and he couldn't believe they had not seen it coming. He had an innate sense about flying. Vernon called it the bird in him saying he was an evolutionary throwback to an earlier species. As they took off in the helicopter, Garland knew a storm would hit over the Cochabamba Range. Luckily, Doug Henry's lodge was just before the peak and might be out of the storm. As Marko and Mei-Ling watched the skies, Garland carefully flew and watched the instruments. They arrived near the lodge coming through the canyon recognized by Marko. They climbed higher and Marko pointed to the ledge where he had stashed the supplies when coming up the hill. Garland also saw it but wanted a better landing place and climbed higher. He suddenly rose over the top and was whipped by the wind. Immediately he lowered the copter behind a row of rocks then carefully worked his way to the yard. All the animals were running so Garland landed quickly and turned off the engine.

As the noise and swirls of dirt calmed down, Marko looked at the big porch and there was Doug rocking in his favorite chair. He stood up and walked toward the group getting out of the helicopter.

"Boy! You really know how to make an entrance, don't you?"

Marko walked ahead grabbing Doug in a hug. "Old man, good to see you again."

"What is all this?" Doug looked at Mei-Ling, immediately taking in the artificial leg and Garland's Texan look. "What gives?"

"Where are Romero and Nissa?" Marko asked.

"Oh, they're waiting inside; I figured you'd make a

mess of the animals. Helicopters don't mix well with the mountains. How did it go, did you hit the storm?"

Garland answered, "Not yet, but we need to move fast to get back beyond the river before it comes over the mountain."

Doug nodded and said, "I'm glad you know what you're doing, I'll get them."

"Can Romero sit or do we need the stretcher?" Garland asked.

"Do you have one? It might be helpful and allow enough room for the others."

"Good idea. I'll get it out of the side door. I don't have the plastic cover so we'll need to wrap him tightly. Some protection over his head due to the cold will help with the rain we'll probably encounter." Garland said.

They all moved quickly and within five minutes Romero was comfortably loaded on the side and they were ready for takeoff.

"Here we go," Doug said, "I never thought I would do this again. I hope you are as good as you sound," shaking his finger at Garland.

"We'll see. Let's make this good. I've arranged to land on the roof of the Rio Branco Hospital." Garland added, "Here we go, everybody lock-in."

They flew without incidence to the hospital and were met by emergency personnel. Connie had managed to arrive a few minutes before the helicopter and greeted them as well. He accompanied Romero into the hospital and took care of the arrangements.

Garland laughed and said, "Connie always amazes

me when he turns up, but I really should be accustomed to this reappearance trick he pulls."

The helicopter took off going back to the Velgrove Estate. Doug and Nissa were given their own lodge room. Neither had brought extra clothes, but soon were being offered clothing to change into so they could take part in the meetings. Marko laughed and shook his head. He had expected Doug to rebel at the inclusion. He was surprised his old friend cooperated with every move as if he had never left civilization to go live alone in the mountains. It entered Marko's mind that perhaps Doug was missing his past.

Everyone freshened up, ate lunch and was ready for the two o'clock meeting.

Connie began, "Hopefully you have had time to read the outline. Let me know what you think and what you think I missed. I had lots of help with this so I have lotsa other people to lay the blame on, so don't hesitate telling me. I won't admit I made the mistake anyway."

They all laughed. Connie had broken the ice again. He always did it. The other brothers expected it.

Doug was not in the meeting. The driver had taken Nissa and him back to check on Romero at the hospital.

Marko started, "Connie, brothers, I would request that we hire or offer to hire Doug Henry to assist with our deliberations and negotiations into the backgrounds of people of interest. He is the expert we have needed. He gave me indications he may be ready to return to duty, just not with the government."

Farimo nodded and spoke, "If he could coordinate

the three groups we are operating, the Boston Analysis Group (BAG), the Qatar Terrorist Analysis Group (Q-TAG) and the Horizon Group we could go back to running our businesses. We can't just stop, or at least I can't."

Chung added, "We need someone we can trust. I think that's why we haven't moved on to this scenario of delegating these duties before now. We have all been waiting for the right person. Marko seems to think Doug Albert Henry is the right one. I respect Marko's analysis of the man."

Garland chimed in, "Here, here. Sounds like, we're in agreement for once."

Chung said, "Thank you for this addition. I was concerned we would have to get some unknown quantity."

Farimo observed, "Essentially your outline says we will become public in all our companies. We, or you Connie, will start a media campaign to discredit the al Qa'ida and others who create terrorist acts. Then the topper to all is we use our influence to manipulate the world economy in conjunction with the Paris Club."

"Connie, what exactly is the Paris Club?" Garland asked.

"Garlie, the Paris Club is known as an informal group of official creditors whose role is to find coordinated and sustainable solutions to the payment difficulties of debtor countries. As debtor countries undertake reforms stabilizing and restoring their macroeconomic and financial situation, Paris Club creditors provide an appropriate debt treatment. Paris Club creditors make available debt treatments to debtor countries in the form of rescheduling, which is debt relief by postponement or, in the case of concessional rescheduling, reduction in debt service obligations during a defined period or a set date. Since 1956, the debt treated in the framework of Paris Club agreements amounts to $553 billion. What this does is make the poorer countries less susceptible to making decisions based on their lack of money, food, jobs and all the other things to be bought. In April 2006, Nigeria became the first African country to fully pay off its debt estimated at $30 billion owed to the Paris Club. Other countries have made payoffs in recent years."

Farimo suggested, "Egypt obtained a $2.2 billion loan from the World Bank after Mubarak resigned."

"More and more, like us, businesses are going multinational. The erosion of America's fundamental economics eroded the nation's trade deficits from $600 to $800 billion escalating the U.S. from the world's leading creditor to largest debtor, reducing bargaining leverage with foreign leaders and costs U.S. 710 million jobs. If we can make the U.S. economy stronger with our outline, the rest of the world will go with us. In every other country in the world corporations are chartered or incorporated nationally applying essential terms of organization, responsibility and performance. Congress should compel all corporations operating in the U. S. be chartered by the federal government."

Garland interrupted, "Congress can't even agree on

the Budget. All those states won't give up the little bit of revenue for creating a corporation. They will scream bloody murder."

"Not if we make it look attractive. We can make it a business by business choice and soon it will be necessary if you want to be successful. These changes are what our companies can do to make changes in thought, philosophy, standards and yes, world economy. I believe it will help each and every one of our companies and influence others to make similar decisions," Connie concluded.

Chung stood. That always meant the meeting was about to be over. "We have until Saturday to think about this. We'll vote then. Have a restful few vacation days. We'll meet here again on Saturday at 2:00pm."

Each family enjoyed the surroundings, took short trips to the ecology biosphere, locations of interest and discussed the future of their companies. On Saturday it was a unanimous vote to go with Connie's outline.

CHAPTER 28
GARLAND RINGS THE WORLD COURT

"Phyllis, where is that old phone book I used to carry?"

"Garland, honey, it's always in your middle desk drawer. You never move it from there."

"I need to call Joseph Wolfhorn. Oh here it is. I pushed it back under some stuff."

Phyllis came in and sat on his desk. "What are you doing? Who are you calling?"

"I'm calling Joseph Wolfhorn. He's that guy I told you about who was a second-year student at the University of Sydney..."

"Oh I remember. I really liked his wife."

"As I was saying, when a friend of his, the fencing team captain, Rupert Brightly asked if he wanted to go to Melbourne the next day to fence in the national university championships, he said, 'You've got to be mad. I've never fenced in my life.' Rupert wasn't crazy, just desperate. A member of the team had fallen ill and they needed a replacement to qualify for the event. Even with his losses, the team won the championship.

And Joe stuck with fencing for years, eventually fencing in the 1956 Olympics and becoming President of the World Bank, a position he held for ten years. He's always been on my short list of people I want to be like when I grow up. I'm still working on it."

"So what's the pattern behind Joe's success?"

"When most people explore an opportunity, next step, or decision, they ask, 'Will I succeed?' But Joe asks a different question, 'Is it worth the risk?' The difference in those questions is the difference between never fencing at all and fencing in the Olympics. When Rupert asked Joe to fence in the championships, there's no chance he could have succeeded. Failure was the inevitable outcome. But was it worth the risk? For Joe, it was. Joe's approach to life is to take a risk, learn from it, and take his new knowledge and understanding to the next risk. Failure is an essential part of his strategy."

Phyllis was skeptical, "He likes failure?"

"Oh, no! Taking risks requires failing. You have to fear failure enough to work hard, making the risks pan out successfully, but not so much that you don't take the risks in the first place. Viewed through the learning lens, failure is as beneficial as success. Look at Connie, if he hadn't failed on the big film, he would not have become the businessman he is today. Working only on things you're pretty sure will work, significantly limits what you can achieve. Instead, take risks and then see what happens."

"What do you expect Joe to help you with?"

"After serving as President of the World Bank, Joe

was asked by President George W. Bush to be the Special Envoy for Gaza Disengagement in the Middle East. If he had asked, "Will it work?" he would never have agreed to tackle that task. Instead, he asked the only question that matters — 'Is it worth the risk?' — and took the job. I believe he will have some answers to my questions concerning the interaction of the poor countries and the moneyed countries."

"Is it true we're focusing on building the economy of African countries?" Phyllis asked.

"Yes, that's right."

Garland dialed the phone and asked for Joseph Wolfhorn. They talked about old times for a few minutes then Garland asked him to have lunch later that day. As he hung up the phone, he nodded his head and said, "This is going to work. He is in limbo, I can tell."

"You think we can get him to help us?" Phyllis asked.

Garland winked and said, "It just might be possible."

Garland called Marko and asked him to join them for lunch at a restaurant on 34th Street in Soho. When the three men arrived, they talked about the weather and their trip to Bolivia for a few minutes then launched into the reason for the meeting. Garland started, "The Velgrove businesses plan to invest money into poor countries who need their economies pumped-up some. Our existing manufacturers will trade with the new companies. This should make the small companies better or it might bring down the already good companies. It's an impossible balancing act. We need someone to coordinate the programs. Are you busy or do you need a challenge?"

Joe answered, "You know I like a challenge. What are you guys into anyway?"

Marko started to explain, "We're using Macro-econometric modeling consisting of behavioral equations and identities of the various interrelationships. These frameworks portray the structure of an economy. The results provide a systematic explanation of how the economy works. Such a model can be validated empirically and used for simulating the effects of policy changes and also provide comprehensive historical accounts of macro-econometric modeling. It would be relevant to note that economic and econometric models reflect the way people actually behave, rather than the way they ought to, which provides a very strong rationale in favor of serious macro-econometric modeling exercises in both developing and developed economies."

Joe continued, "The Input-Output model is an adaptation of the neo-classical theory of general equilibrium to the empirical analysis of interdependence between different activities. Leontief's Input-Output table is essentially a detailed account of the inter-relationships that exist among various sectors of an economy. An article by Leontief on Input-Output relationships in the US economy marked the beginning of this major branch of quantitative economics. Yes, guys I know about the Input-Output system. What are we going to do with it?"

Garland grabbed his hand and shook it. "Joe welcome aboard. You're practically a Velgrove, anyway."

Marko continued, "We're using the Input-Output models, incorporating pricing, forecasting and planning. Multiregional Input-Output (MRIO) model that introduces significant improvements for the estimate of trade flows between the regions – a key element in all international models. We will confirm the position of negative trade balance in relation to all the other macro regions, indicating a significant dependence of this area on the Center-North. The economic system impact on lower areas, even allowing for productive technology differences using the fabrication globally only partially generates local economy effects, while triggering production in other geographical areas."

Joe was fascinated by the conversation and said, "At one job I spent time following the quantitative comparison with bi-regional models developed in previous studies. The dependence of economy in terms of trade balance and production trigger has always been noted. A comparison takes into consideration the four macro regions bringing evidence a general increase in the volume of multiregional trade starts closing the gap in relation to multiregional trade, and increasing integration with the macro region. The analysis of the backward and the forward linkages, applied to the regions instead of sectors confirms the key regions sell a lower amount of intermediate products and thus have low links with other regions. One last methodological observation is the different behavior emerging from the analyses triggering economic macro areas. While a national model may be strongly conditioned by the regions, a model of a multiregional and multi-sector type can take into consideration the interrelations existing between all elements of a dualistic system."

Garland looked at the two men and said, "I haven't the faintest idea what you guys are talking about. I just know you will do the best."

Marko continued, "Let's talk about practicalities. My building has a couple of empty offices perhaps you could set-up there until we get this whole thing going."

"I would like that. At the end of the month I need to take a short trip to my daughter's graduation." Joe continued, "My wife is looking forward to driving up the coast to Yale."

"Phyllis will be really happy to see your wife again they got on well back in the Netherlands when you were there." Garland added.

Marko said, "You two may want to catch-up. I need to be getting back to the office. It was great meeting you Joe. I look forward to seeing you in the office. Here's a card, call me when you are on your way."

"I'll be there in about an hour to set up a few things and then I'll come in tomorrow morning."

"You really are amazing, and get going fast," Garland said.

As Marko left he was shaking his head at the speed of Joe's cooperation. Marko started thinking of all the preparations he must make to prepare Joe's office. As he walked back to Velgrove Industries, he called Rosalyn.

By the time he got to the office she had checked the facility and made it ready to occupy. He was still astounded at how much she knew and could handle on her own, if he just let her do it. When people started giving her directions, she took her time carrying out every detail.

As he walked the air seemed to change. He looked up at the blue slice between the buildings. Summer would be here soon. Maybe he could take Mei-Ling to the Bahamas for a few days, rent a boat and sail in the islands. As he rounded the corner, Connie was entering the Velgrove building. Marko thought, "I didn't know he was coming today."

"Hey, Connie, what's going on?" Marko greeted his uncle.

Connie turned in front of the elevator and shook Marko's hand while saying, "Glad you're here. I wasn't sure. We need to talk and make some plans."

"Good, I have updates for you also. Garland and I just had lunch with Joe Wolfhorn. Do you know him?"

"Sure! That's a good idea. I assume you were offering him a job."

"Well, Garland put that in motion. I had little to do with it." Marko added. "They seem to be old friends. Phyllis was involved in a business with his wife when they were in The Netherlands. They did some projects together."

"We're moving fast on this African plan. How

would your Input-Output Group feel about traveling in Africa?"

"I would imagine they'd think it was a plus. They don't travel much, just computer work."

"Give'em a break and send them over to survey all the Africa countries. We'll start in Cape Town, South Africa and move on to the southern three countries, Botswana, Lesotho, Namibia who may have information we can use," Connie was talking as they arrived in his office where he set-up his New York crew. "If we make appointments for them to be visiting professors at the local college or university they will have the local stats available and can get input from the students as well."

"I can see how that would work. Actually it's a great idea. Let me get Rosalyn in here to take notes."

Marko walked down the hallway and spoke to Rosalyn, put his coat in his office and checked his messages. By the time he returned, Connie and Rosalyn were discussing the reservations and travel arrangements to be made.

As he came into the room Marko said, "Remember, this past week they were all attending the Society for International Development World Congress. It was held in Washington, D.C. so I thought it would have information and contacts they could utilize."

Connie looked up and asked, "When is that over?"

"It was over August 31st. They should have a week back in Boston before they go away again. They can do most of the work online, but on short notice we'll need to clear-up what's come in during that week they were gone."

"That'll work fine. I can get them there in about two weeks for the first appearance in Cape Town, South Africa. Remember summertime in Africa happens in a few months, will make it easier to get fill-in professorships for our group."

CHAPTER 29
INPUT-OUTPUT GOES TO AFRICA

The Velgrove company jet flew from New York to Stuttgart where they picked up the European group members and headed to Cape Town, South Africa. Joe Wolfhorn was briefing Malcolm Williamson, Jerome Silva, Jeannette Rothman and the new additions to the Input-Output team from The Netherlands, Janis Oostersteen and Orville Katasuma, from Japan. He was reviewing the planned speeches and trying to anticipate the many questions likely to be posed afterward.

"Before we get started, does everyone know each other?" Joe asked.

They all said they did but did not know the man in back or the woman with him.

Joe stated, "This is Douglas Albert Henry, ex-US Treasury agent who will be known to you as Doug. He will be arranging your security so get to know him well. The woman with him probably has spoken, to many of you from time to time. She is Cindy Bartell of the Qatar Security Group."

The statisticians nodded and said simultaneously,

"That makes sense. Yes I know her, but never saw her in person before."

After the introductions were finished Joe started, "Our plan is to obtain as much cooperation as possible while collecting information concerning the economic variants of each country we visit. In your folders, you will find an outline from the CIA World Fact Book website, which you may want to reference occasionally for further initial information about the various countries."

"We are splitting you into teams. Each team will cover both different geographic and productivity areas. The universities are welcoming our interest and have been very helpful in making arrangements. Most of you know who your partners and areas are."

As Joe pointed to the papers he continued, "Are you familiar with the CIA website? If not please check it out. The information is simply a starting point. The University of Zambia is the first University. You will arrive there speak then continue on to the University of Cape Town. In the same area are University of Western Cape, Cape Peninsula University of Technology, International Peace University South Africa and University of Stellenbosch University. Janis Oostersteen and Jeannette Rothman will be taking the Southern Area. As we move from country to country we'll try to include the nearby universities with the group meeting. As you know there are several regions in Africa fighting civil wars. Even where the wars have been stopped, there is a heavy degree of hatred prevalent in countries who have not settled their differences. Due to previous wars it will be difficult for us to accomplish our goals. Nothing is without a solution. We will make the best effort possible."

"Please read your material and I hope you are as excited as I am. This is an earth changing project. You should be proud to be included. You are the starters, many others will follow you. If we are successful we will lay the ground work for a better world economy. Thank you for having the courage to participate in this new beginning."

"From a macro-econometric set-up I recommended we divide the African countries using geographic area, growth rate, and exports and imports. If we start with geographic you have four distinct areas – The southern area contains South Africa, Zimbabwe, Namibia, Botswana, Mozambique, Angola, Zambia, Tanzania and Madagascar. The other areas are Midlands or Equatorial, Desert, Western and there is a fifth area along the Gulf of Aden and Canal – Somalia, Djibouti, Sudan, and Egypt. These four countries are also part of other geographic areas. The economies of these countries share in either Suez Canal revenues or shipping service activities connected with the country's strategic locations and status as a free trade zone in the Horn of Africa."

"Our third main stop will be the University of Nairobi, Kenya. They have a Department of Environmental and Biosystems Engineering on Harry Thuku Road, Nairobi City, Kenya. We will spend three days there setting-up classes and projects to be carried out by the students. This is the Midlands or Equatorial Area. I suggest we make a decision to call it Equatorial."

Jeannette spoke up, "Joe, we have some information from the East African Tea Trade Association."

"I am not acquainted with that company."

Jeannette continued, "It isn't a company but an association of about 300 companies. This is a voluntary organization of Tea Producers, Buyers, Exporters, Brokers, Tea Packers and Warehouses. All entities are working to promote the best interests of the Tea Trade in Africa. Currently, membership comprises over three hundred companies extending across the East and Central African borders. It sounds like what we are looking to do with a variety of companies."

Joe beamed, "This is exactly the type of information we need to further plan the Velgrove interactions. Keep your eyes open for Associations such as this one. They could also be called cooperatives, guilds, federation, society, syndicate, alliance, conglomerate, co-op or fellowship. As we move through Africa, we will collect old projects already completed. We will honor their initiatives and encourage future projects to make a difference in their country. When we add to these figures the investment by Velgrove Industries International, NY, Inc. you will see a tremendous difference in the amount of trade and industry in the cooperating countries."

Jeannette added, "The East African Tea Trade Association is also across country borders. There are at lease five countries in different geographic areas in the association."

"This is beginning to look interesting. We will see cooperation across the lines we draw. That only makes our job more interesting, right? There will be non-cooperating countries also. In those countries we may be able to start a cooperating group within the country to act as a demonstrating yardstick showing how a little planning can work for the benefit of all. We may want to go across geographic areas also."

Mal Williamson asked, "The work we've done shows several of the countries would be reticent to accept help from the West. How does that fit into our overall plan?"

"Well, Mal, that is the beauty of the plan Connie and the other brothers have worked out. We will be investing from within their region and not around the world. It will look more like a give and take, import/export situation not humanitarian aid from the World Food Programme. If a country can raise enough food and maintain mining, manufacturing or tourism they will have enough diverse economy to sustain the GDP for their people. What we are doing is pairing poor countries with already sustainable countries in hopes they will benefit each other." Joe continued.

"Jeannette, it sounds to me as if you would make a good fit in the Equatorial Area. Orville, by the way how did you get that name in Kyoto?"

Orville answered, "My mother watched television a lot and liked popcorn."

The group laughed. Then Joe continued, "Okay, Orville, would you continue on the Equatorial Area team with Jeannette as your partner?"

"Sure, boss, I be glad to work with most good looking person in the room."

They all laughed at Orville's joking around. It broke the seriousness of the atmosphere.

"That means we need someone to join Janis in the south."

Jerome Silva spoke up, "I've done previous work in the southern area and have a thing about the Boers. I find them interesting, in spite of their prejudices."

Joe considered the decision and said, "If that is your interest, we'll do it. You and Janis need to spend about a month traveling around in the Southern Area."

Mal Williamson spoke up, "I guess that leaves you and me, Dude. You almost sound like the Afrikaners. If I take all the little countries in the Western Coastal Area, can you do the deserts?"

Joe answered, "I have my work cut out for me. I am contacting every government in Africa – all countries. I will be doing 'glad handing', delving into their laws and asking questions of each country's leaders. Dora has offered two more of the input-output statisticians who have to finish their projects before leaving. Jordon Smith and Conrad Nagle will be arriving in Egypt next week. Adella Abba will coordinate their trip and introduce them to the universities."

Mal Williamson commented, "I guess I'm on my own, then."

"We figured you could handle it. You will be able to convince people and if not, we will give you some help. You will be doing the statistics on the growth and Input-Output of the various countries. We will then decide which ones to pare-up with and demonstrate our policies. We will be in Lusaka, Zambia in a few hours. I'm afraid once we hit the ground we will be busy every minute. Please try to rest for the next few hours and be ready. This may be the biggest challenge of your life. Thank you for being a participant."

Joe sat down, turned his head to the porthole and tried to sleep. He was so excited he could not. This was the culmination of all the work he had tried to do earlier at the World Bank and Israel. Tomorrow this team would start gathering the information, next analyze it and act upon its indicators.

CHAPTER 30
BROTHERS USE THE
INFORMATION

Jordan Smith and Conrad Nagle finished their data collection with Adella Abba's help. She made the work easier by coordinating meeting sequences and distances of trips to the eleven Desert Area countries. She assembled statisticians in the Cairo offices. Each night the travelers sent their additional information to the Abba Industries, Ltd. offices to be assembled and worked over by her two sons who were learning the business from their parents.

By the time Jordan and Conrad returned, the information was already beginning to make sense. The Desert Area economies were based mostly on hydrocarbons, subsistence farming or nomadic livestock, phosphates and very little manufacturing. Only one of the countries had moved into the twenty-first century with electronics. Egypt and Morocco are dependent on tourism and Somalia has the lowest wireless telecommunication rates for the continent and together with Morocco has mastered money transfer/remittance services.

As the statisticians worked they laid out the Input-Output tables and interrelationships. Jordan and Conrad returned to the Boston Office as other members of the team arrived in Cairo with more and more data. Farimo had installed mainframe computers but as Mal Williamson said, "Dude, we've been working with our laptops for so long we've solved the memory problem. We just keep plugging in more raid drives and eventually we can compute any problem. If you tie enough raids together you can do anything."

Farimo answered, "We will run the numbers on the big computers after you finish with your preliminaries."

Hosni Abba, Farimo and Adele's son said, "Dad, don't worry the mainframe will be necessary in the long run."

After going to the University of Texas in Austin, Hosni had only been back in Egypt for a few months but was so computer trained he could do any job required. He worked in Alexandria for a hardware manufacturer, Wissam, whose business was mainly innovative design & manufacturing electronics equipment and systems. Hosni moved quickly from part designer to teacher in the electronic school.

When his father called saying he needed a good electronics assembly guy to run computers in the office, Hosni questioned the challenge of working in his father's company and was not sure he should leave his job, but his Mother asked and he could never refuse her. After all she had allowed him to follow his desire to learn computers in the first place. His brother Andre had already worked several years for the company and vouched for the authenticity of the job. Andre told Hosni, "Dad and mom have one of the most challenging, earth-shaking and by the way, disturbing projects I've ever heard about, much less worked on."

His father had always wanted him to go into the oil business, the family's best money maker, and his father wanted to keep that part of Abba Industries, Ltd. healthy. Nagilii the oldest son had been living and working in Abu Dhabi studying the banking and oil businesses since he returned from Harvard three years ago. He visited his mother and father frequently and had been there for the first few weeks of Marko's initiation trip.

Joe Wolfhorn finally arrived in Cairo. He had visited every African country's government. Some were helpful and encouraged development. Other side of the coin was no interest and downright belligerence at the thought of assistance or teaching what to do for their country. Joe was tired and looked harried. Adella and Farimo did their best to entertain him and could not understand his seemingly deep depression. Finally they had to concede he was just tired.

He bought an outrageous diamond from Adella's mine, had it set for his wife and left for New York.

A few days after he returned to his office in New York, Marko met Joe going down the hall and asked about his wife, the diamond and questioned Joe about his health.

"Joe, you didn't catch one of those bugs out there in

the real world, did you?" Marko asked.

"No, no, I'm just run down. I'll get rested in a few more days."

Marko made a mental note to check on him in a couple of days; however the brothers were coming to town for deliberation on the Input-Output results. By the time Marko saw Joe again he looked even gaunter and had a sallow complexion. Marko suggested Joe take a few days off and check with a doctor. They all overlooked the warnings while the meeting got going.

When Connie and Garland argued it was always time consuming. Finally Chung would declare what they should do, but that didn't stop the questions this time. They had been arguing for four days straight. They were making decisions governing their actions for the next ten to twenty years, maybe more. As Farimo said, "I feel like we should be listening to our children this time. They are the ones who will have to live with the decisions we make this week."

Chung said, "You're right Farimo. All of you send for your children. Have them sit in on the meeting on Friday. All of them must be here and their wives or husbands. This must be a family decision. My son, his wife and my grandson will be here and of course Mei-Ling and Marko have already been part of the deliberations."

So they had two days rest from arguments, while the next generation of Velgroves arrived.

S.F. Lee was the first to make his presence felt. He demanded to see all the 'so called' arrangements. He came with his entourage as usual and stayed at the most prestigious hotel in New York. He had married Su-Ing Ho, the daughter of the Macau banking family. They had a son, but she kept a constant watch on her husband. She ran a casino in Macau and Masqat, Oman. He had time to gamble and play the bigwig. She told him early in their marriage, "Never, never embarrass the Ho Family. You won't live to regret it."

S.F. had become more controlled in his actions and let her control the money and businesses. He was a figure head who took her every where she went. She was at the meeting in New York also. She listened to all the proposals, let S.F. make belligerent comments to Marko and Connie. The whole charade was almost more than Chung Kee Lee could stand. He was not in charge and felt useless.

During the late afternoon, Su-Ing Ho rose and spoke, "The work done by Marko Fushier and Joseph Wolfhorn is of utmost quality and creates final decisions easily. The Lee International Casinos would like to negotiate installing areas of tourism in the countries outlined by your project. We will build six hotels where specified by the plans. When you are ready for tourism to increase, please let me know."

Chung looked at his son and rose to speak, "Thank you for taking part in the planning. We are all better for your ideas."

S.F. rose, took his wife's arm, motioned to the entourage and left the room.

As the elevator door closed, he struck his wife on the

face and said, "Don't ever embarrass me in front of my father again."

She was stunned and motioned to the bodyguard to stand back. Raymond and the bodyguard took a separate taxi to the hotel. When Raymond arrived he went straight to the bar where S.F. sat with a drink. The bodyguard stood by the door. Raymond whispered, "Charlie, have you lost your mind?"

"I'm tired of it. I won't take it anymore." S.F. yelled.

"But, Charlie, her family is so powerful. When she appears with a black eye, her brother will blow his top. You know that. Please apologize," Raymond pleaded.

"I don't care anymore," S.F. yelled.

The bodyguard walked over and put his arm around S.F. and squeezed his shoulder. S.F. crumpled and the guard said, "Come on with me to your suite."

The two left toward the elevator while Raymond sat in the bar and finished his drink. He went to his room thinking, "Charlie will call soon."

Charlie didn't call soon. Su-Ing Ho left the hotel within the hour and flew to Macau.

As Charlie/S.F. walked to his room his uncle, Connie, was coming towards him with his bodyguard, Moody. They each took an arm and took Charlie into the connecting hallway. As they walked, Connie started talking.

"I understand you had a little temper tantrum this afternoon, Charlie. You know the Ho family will be after you and most likely will kill you in a most painful way."

"Oh, Connie, I don't care. Everything I had has evaporated. Just let them kill me. Then it will all be over."

"No. Your father saved my life. I owe him something. He does not deserve to lose you like this. Moody here is going to take you to Bolivia and you will work with the Velgrove Corps Group. If you are inclined or are good enough we will put you in charge of the Oil Drilling Group in a country of your choice. You need to toughen up before it's too late for you."

Moody had a van waiting behind the hotel, rushed Charlie to the airport and the waiting Velgrove Plane. They flew to Miami and refueled again in Panama City before ending in Rurrenabaque. He was taken to the training field and started on an intense development program.

He dropped the F.S. and became just Chuck Chung. He was on his own for the first time in his life. He was treated as an individual, not the son of somebody. He had always resented his father's influence. No one knew who he was and didn't care. He had to stand or fall on his own.

CHAPTER 31
MARKO RETURNS TO NEW YORK

Marko worked with Connie, Garland and Farimo. First he analyzed with Farimo's computers evaluating the numbers gathered by the Input-Output team during their African trip. The I/O group did a remarkable job gathering the information, making and applying the interaction criteria, but Marko had an agenda specified in the Connie Report and approved in the Bolivia Meeting. He applied exchange rates information from the paper written by Utz-Peter Reich, *Inequality in Exchange, The Use of World Trade Flow Table for Analyzing the International Economy*, and *Economic Integration: Systemic Measures in an Input – Output Framework*, by Dipti Prakas Pal, Erik Dietzenbacher and Dipika Basu. Connie and Garland kept him company during this analysis. After Connie argued for the people of an area and Garland argued for the brother's investments. They had argued for years, since Connie traveled to all the areas and Garland kept his head filled with the details of their investments, they each came at a problem from different directions. Farimo had his favorite opinion that included economic modeling for disaster impact analysis. Eventually, they were able to agree on an action plan.

Connie stayed in Thessaloniki after the long month in Cairo. Amanda and Shimon flew to be with him. The work had been intense in Egypt. Connie had been hotheaded and unrelenting. Garland although stubborn, eventually agreed with his brother trying to make concessions producing the campaign Connie had outlined. The brothers finally were able to set aside their differences in concept, putting a plan into action.

Connie felt bad for not telling Chung his son was in South America, but wanted the new, Chuck Chung to present himself to his father later. Amanda, expressing interest in Connie's Film business, had written a script and was interviewing investors for her upcoming movie. Connie thought it was 'cute,' introduced her to some investors but kept out of the negotiations, letting her make her own decisions. She took on the tasks easily.

They were enjoying their life in Thessaloniki. The hospital next door was serving the area people well. Their friends visited from the U.S. and Australia. The movie finally was funded and Amanda was set to go into production in one month. She looked forward to location traveling and production sites making her own movie come to life.

While clothes shopping in the local market one day, she moved from store to store and eventually realized someone was following her. A good looking young man kept standing nearby, looking sideways at what she was doing. At first, she didn't think too much about it, but the man appeared in five other locations. While looking for Moody's number to call on her cell phone she snapped two good views of the person following her. She asked Moody to meet her at the local restaurant.

Amanda waited for Moody while the young man watched from two tables away. When Moody arrived, he acted as if he was assisting her with packages to the car. Another bodyguard had already gone into action. The woman, Ariala, was in great physical condition and sat at the table next to Ahmed Nahbi. Moody had identified him from Amanda's cell phone pictures. Ariala smiled at him, tried to engage him in conversation and was unable to make a connection with him before he suddenly bolted out of the restaurant and disappeared in an alley. The Corps Group was alerted but assumed Ahmed was looking for Mei-Ling. Extra surveillance was put in place for the Kaulas' household.

As Ahmed ran down the alley behind the restaurant he was thinking fast. How could he get out? He didn't expect that woman to be part of the Constantine Kaulas guard squad. How had he been so short sighted and not seen this coming. He had followed Kaulas' wife all day. He was sure she had no awareness of him. How had the guard appeared so quickly? Ahmed got back to the challenge at hand of rescuing himself out of this alley. He ran into an open doorway and climbed the stairs two at a time. He jumped inside a closet and melded into the woodwork. He heard footsteps on the stairs, stayed quiet and waited. About an hour later he slowly opened the door and went to the roof.

The roof was flat and attached to the building next door. He looked at all the surrounding streets and alleys to see if they had a squad waiting. He saw no one waiting. After dark he came out of the building and proceeded to his hotel. He had all the information needed to get to Constantine Kaulas. That smart ass would never see it coming. Kaulas, the Israeli lover, worked with the Greeks too. The Iman in Baabar had followed the smear campaign instigated by Kaulas and had demanded he be stopped. Ahmed had volunteered immediately. He told them how he had almost killed the whole family on the bridge in San Pedro when they were going to the boat. The Spanish kids he hired had not responded quickly enough when he gave the command to explode the Volkswagen on the Vincent Thomas Bridge. The Harbor patrol just didn't know how close they came to blowing an oceangoing ship in the harbor. That would have messed up the traffic flow for months.

Mei-Ling never appreciated what he could do. She was such an intellectual, never realistic. He could have cared for her, but she insulted him in front of his family, so she would have to apologize forever to make up for what she did to him.

He was trained in combat tactics. He could kill a person twenty different ways without leaving a trace. He had done his reconnaissance well. He could rest for two days and take care of Kaulas on the third day. After that he would have fulfilled his atonement and be free to pursue Mei-Ling again without interference from the Iman or his family.

Ahmed started watching the Kaulas house at midnight. After 1:00am he entered the backyard area quietly moving from shadow to shadow until reaching the basement stairs. He entered the basement, slowly edged his way up the back stairs waiting 45 min. at the hallway door until he was sure he could proceed. The evening quiet made every movement echo throughout the house. Ahmed slowly slid on his stomach down the hallway and into the library. This was a tactic spreading the pressure and making it noiseless. Only sliding on the ceiling would have made less intrusion, dream on Ahmed. He secreted himself in a corner closet. He oiled the hinges making them noiseless and made himself comfortable for the wait.

In mid-afternoon, Ahmed was aroused by noises coming from the library. He heard Constantine Kaulas talking to his young son. Ahmed stepped out of the closet and started towards Connie who glanced around and said to his son, "Shimmy this is very important run to mother quickly and close the door. Run! Run! Now, Shimmy!"

Ahmed had time to go behind Connie and slash a rope around his neck before Connie could fight back. Connie's first concern was to get Shimmy out of the room. After accomplishing that it was too late to fight. Ahmed was able to overcome Connie quickly. After strangling his prey, Ahmed made his way out the window he had opened earlier last night and ran for the rode down the hill. He jumped in the car waiting for him, drove to the airport and left on the next flight out.

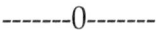

Amanda called Garland frantic at 3:00am Texas time.

"Garland! He said call you."

"Is that you Amanda?" Garland asked.

"Garland, he was in the study working. I heard a noise but didn't think anything was wrong. Shimmy ran to me saying, 'Daddy said come to mommy.' When I took him tea, Connie was dead. He's dead, dead!"

"Darling, what happened?"

"I don't know."

"Who is with you?

"Shimon is here. Oh, you mean others."

"Yes, let me talk to the security."

There was a silence on the phone for seemingly hours before the voice came, "Hello? This is Moody. Who is this?"

"This is Garland Velgrove. I'm sure you know me and I know who and what you do."

"You're right Mr. Velgrove. We have a tragedy here."

"What do you need? I think Amanda and Shimon should come to Austin, Texas and stay on the ranch for awhile. I can have the Corporate Jet there in seven hours. Can you make her safe until then?"

"I can't promise any of that until I investigate. We

are still trying to figure out what happened."

"What can you do to protect her?"

"I have Amanda and Shimon in a safe room. Send the Jet. Send Aaron and his group from Israel. That should give some help. So you will know, someone broke into the study by window and broke his neck," Moody stated.

"Dear God, what are we coming to? Do you have any guess who did this?" Garland said.

Moody continued, "I'm pretty sure it was Ahmed Nahbi or someone he hired. They're gone already. I can't be certain, but I doubt he will strike again at this location."

"I've sent them a message to fly. The plane is on the way."

"We had stalkers three days ago during Amanda's shopping trip. This had to be well planned over a long time. Connie went so many places and he was starting the publicity campaign. He never expected this response in Greece. This was not for his personal promotion this time."

Garland hung up the phone. Phyllis was already by his side. He hugged her and walked into the study, or as he called it, the workroom. He sat at his desk and broke into shuddering sobs. Finally he raised his head and took control of himself, picked up the phone and started making phone calls to Chung, Farimo, Marko, Mei-Ling, Su-Ing Ho and finally Joseph Wolfhorn.

There was a memorial service at the Velgrove Ranch. Connie was buried next to his father and mother. Amanda returned to Los Angeles and to everyone's amazement she started running the International Pictures Studio. She continued with the pictures Connie had planned, the distribution went smoothly and the Industry welcomed her with open arms, seemingly.

The other brothers were not content to just go on with their lives. They each kept constant contact with the security corps and looked for any possibility leading to Connie's killer. Nothing surfaced from their interviews.

Chung was beginning to tire easily and only worked half days. He was sure Charlie was gone forever. Only Connie and Moody knew Charlie was still alive and Moody had many well kept secrets.

Mei-Ling still taught chemistry at NYU, had received a USDA grant to develop agricultural chemicals and was making good progress on the soil replacement nutrients. Finally beginning to feel normal again, she was encouraged by not receiving further emails from Ahmed Nahbi. She assumed he had gone away for further insurgent training.

When the nub of her leg ached, she still thought of Ahmed. She was concentrating on her work when the door opened behind her. Glancing over her shoulder she saw no one. Turning to continue her work, she heard the lock snap closed.

Ahmed had easily found Mei-Ling once he arrived in New York. Getting there was the challenge. He had gone to Mexico City, flown to San Francisco under an assumed name and driven cross-country. The week crossing from west to east coast had acclimated Ahmed to the American ways again. He had forgotten how they trusted everyone. He bought clothes in Omaha so he would look American. He arrived in New York, found a place to stay with other Muslims and started his search for Mei-Ling. The university gave her office address and class schedule over the phone. He followed her for a whole week before he made his move. She went to the lab on Friday morning. When others left at noon, he entered the lab.

Ahmed thought, "She's there alone so what could she do? She's only a woman, who knows chemistry, what could she do against a man like me?"

After entering he lowered himself behind one of the desks, reached over and snapped the door lock. Mei-Ling knew immediately who was there. She stood, removed her prosthesis and sat on the stool again where she continued looking at the chemistry experiment. In her left hand she held the most effective weapon available the metal foot.

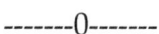

Ahmed knew nothing of her foot amputation.

That morning Marko had returned from yet another trip to Cairo, he called Mei-Ling's office and got her Asian secretary who said, "Miss Mei-Ling spending today at the lab and said no disturbing except you. What surprise you are returned, Mr. Marko."

"Yes, I'm a few days early. I'll just walk over and drop into the lab about lunch time."

"That would be nice."

As Marko hung up the phone he couldn't wait to see Mei-Ling, but he looked at his desk, opened a few letters and before he realized, it was eleven thirty, so he bolted outside and grabbed a taxi. As he leaned back for the ride he closed his eyes and meditated. After a minute the Cougar appeared, staring into the night of his mind the big cat lunged at him. Marko jumped and grunted so loud the driver hit the brakes. Marko said, "Hurry, hurry. I need to get there fast."

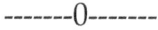

-------0-------

Marko handed the driver a fifty dollar bill saying, "Floor it. It's an emergency."

Ahmed continued crawling across the floor between the lab desks. Mei-Ling said, "Ahmed, I know it's you."

"You dirty bitch! I'll kill you today just like your uncle Constantine."

"Just keep on slithering across the floor like the snake you are, Ahmed."

"You filthy whore, you'd fuck anything."

"Tell me about Uncle Connie."

"I showed him. He thought he could slander my people."

"Ahmed, your people are using you. They're making you do things you would never do on your own."

He jumped up and started running toward Mei-Ling, yelling, "Whore! Bitch! You will pay for your whoring."

As he lunged toward Mei-Ling, she swung the metal appendage while turning on the lab stool where she sat. As she turned, the metal foot caught a bottle of nitric acid on the desk. It flew off splashing across Ahmed's face and arm as he ran toward her. She jumped from the stool, fell to the floor and crawled to the opposite side of the desk.

When he stumbled and hit the floor, the bottle broke and splashed more. He couldn't see.

She only had a few splatters so pulled up and washed the acid from her arms and hands.

Ahmed screamed continuously until he passed out and lay still. Mei-Ling waited. After a few minutes she heard knocking on the door she started rolling toward the door and yelled, "Call the Fire Department!"

Mei-Ling stopped talking when Ahmed stood and lunged at the sound she made.

He screamed again and collapsed before he reached her position behind the next lab desk. The students came for their lab at 1:00pm, she waited, surely it must be almost time. He was moving around again.

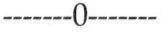

The driver floored it and wildly went through the traffic. In ten minutes they arrived at the lab. Marko jumped out and waved the cabbie to go. Running across the grass and into the Chemistry building, Marko tripped but kept on running. As he reached the hallway there were people crowd at the end of the corridor pointing and talking to some firemen. Marko ran into the middle of the crowd and yelled, "What's wrong? What happened?"

"The lab is locked and the person inside will not open."

"I have to get my experiment finished today and this happens."

The fireman said, "Don't worry we'll get you in there soon. As soon as my partner returns we will have help. It would help if you would stand at the other end of the corridor. Just in case. We don't want some other experiment to go awry, now do we?"

Marko peered through the small glass in the door, but couldn't see anything, except some steam on the other side of the room. He stretched and finally saw Mei-Ling's prosthetic spring foot at the edge of the counter. He turned to the fireman and asked, "Are there any outside windows? My wife is in there on the floor."

"We can get in right through here in a minute." As he talked Marko saw firemen coming in the front door with equipment and running through the crowded hall. They stopped and took out an axe and broke the glass. One stuck his hand in and unlocked the door. Marko pushed in with the firemen and ran to Mei-Ling. She rolled over and said, "Get down he's over there."

Marko pulled her around the desk edge and put his

body over hers. The firemen walked over to the smoke and gasped. Ahmed was on the floor with nitric acid all over his face and hands writhing in pain in a pool of blood and his face and hands melted down to the bone.

When Marko knew it was safe to move her, he carried Mei-Ling to the hallway and was met by a fireman with a stretcher. As he gently laid her on it he was looking for injuries but saw none.

When Marko went back into the lab to retrieve her spring foot lying under the desk, he saw Ahmed fighting with the firemen. Marko retrieved the foot and came back. The fireman quickly moved her down the hallway out the front door and into a waiting ambulance. As they drove to the hospital Marko asked, "Darling, what happened?"

She told Marko about the attack as they drove to the hospital in the ambulance with sirens screaming.

Mei-Ling was treated by the University Hospital Emergency room and released. As they walked toward the exit, police officers stopped them and asked to speak about what had occurred. Mei-Ling told the story again and added that Ahmed had been at UCLA while she was and by drugging he had taken her to Lebanon. The policemen not able to comprehend all the information finally realized they were in over their heads. Marko and Mei-ling were asked to come to the police station on campus.

Mei-Ling told the story to the campus police, the NYPD, the FBI and maybe some more police who didn't exactly identify themselves. After five or six more times, they left to go home.

As they walked into their apartment Marko picked her up into his arms and carried her across the transom saying, "This is our home and I want you to marry me. I know we can't have children, but I don't want to live without you as my partner, lover, companion and most of all, my wife."

"Oh my darling, I thought you would never ask me."

"Will you marry me?"

"Yes, of course."

After calling all the brothers, Amanda Kaulas and Su-Ing Ho with the news, they spent the weekend getting to know each other again. Several reporters called and wanted an interview. When Ahmed Nahbi died of his wounds the reporters called again trying to get her to talk to them. Marko called the phone company and changed the number and ordered new cell phones. They drove to Newport and spent a day of peaceful leisure. They walked on the beach and for the first time Mei-ling saw the Fushier family home. They didn't stay there because it had been closed for three years now and he wanted comfort for this one weekend.

The next morning Mei-Ling was lying awake staring at the ceiling when Marko opened his eyes. She said, "I've been planning our wedding."

"Tell me, tell me." Marko said.

"We'll have the whole family fly in to Los Angeles. We'll go to the REGAL SONJIA and have the captain marry us on the way to Catalina where we will have a celebration and be with our family."

"What a marvelous plan," Marko said as he hugged her.

CHAPTER 32
VELGROVES RETURN TO CATALINA

The Family leased two vacation houses on Catalina Island for the month of July. The weather was beautiful. The clouds of June had been pushed out to sea and left the sunny 70 to 80 degree temperatures. Mei-Ling finished the quarter at NYU and traveled to Los Angeles the last week in June. She carried her wedding dress packed and ready to go to the REGAL SONJIA where she stayed making arrangements for the arrival of the family.

Marko flew to Los Angeles and stayed in the Dan Quail Suite of Ritz Carlton in Marina del Rey. The suite consumes the whole top floor and has a fabulous view of the Pacific Ocean. There were rooms for the whole Velgrove family there but the DQ Suite was reserved for the Fushiers and Scotts. Marko's uncle, the ambassador who took his father's place in Argentina was there as well as his mother's sister, Sally Anne Scott. These people and their families stayed with Marko in the DQ Suite. The REGAL SONJIA docked at the California Yacht Club next door to the hotel.

The Families went onboard the yacht, taking their luggage and gifts for the bride. Garland and Phyllis and their two daughters, Geraldine and Jacqueline were the first to arrive. Then Amanda with Shimon came but had no luggage because she had sent it ahead to the vacation house on Catalina. The Lee's had been on the boat for the previous week in San Pedro. Mei-Ling's mother had been there for a month making arrangements with the wedding planner, decorating the stateroom on the boat they would use as a wedding chapel and enjoying the opportunity to prepare her daughter's wedding. Mei-Ling knew her mother would take over so she just relaxed and enjoyed the occasion.

The big surprise was Joe Wolfhorn and his wife. Joe had finally gone to the doctor and was being treated for a rare disease contracted while in Africa. He looked like a new person, vibrant and lively again.

The Abba family arrived only that morning in the private jet at LAX. They went straight to the Yacht Club and boarded with Chung Lee and Nila. S.F. Chung's wife, Su-Ing Ho of Macau and their son, Chico were there. Everyone was dressed for the wedding.

Marko and the Fushiers arrived at the boat and REGAL SONJIA left for Catalina Island. After leaving everyone was seated in the stateroom when the music changed to the wedding march Mei-Ling came through the door and everyone gasped. She was in an ecru sleek sheath with orchids cascading down the front. She elegantly walked to the alter and kneeled with Marko. The ship's captain, Hi Shu, repeated the vows and they added a prayer of their own and were pronounced man and wife.

Every one congratulated them and there was champagne for all. Some food was served, but they waited for the banquet to be served at the restaurant on Catalina Island where the brothers had taken Marko to be part of the family. The Casino Dock Café was reserved for the Velgrove family today. It seemed like twenty years ago. It had been only one year and a few months since the first dinner.

The families reveled in the happiness of the couple and as the night moved on they left to go on to their own lives again. Marko and Mei-Ling would have a short honeymoon on the REGAL SONJIA, but the others stayed on Catalina in the vacation houses until returning to work again.

Several days into their leisurely cruise, Marko and Mei-Ling were lounging in bed one morning when a knock on the door startled them. The sailors had left them alone and not interacted at all.

"There is a call for Mr. Fushier in the radio room." The sailor said.

Marko hurriedly dressed and went up top to talk. "Sorry Marko, I know you don't want to hear this but we need to move on the African project. There is concern for another rebellion in Kenya. We need to consistently institute the plans worked out in your Input-Output survey. Joe has flown to Kampala, Uganda and will move on to Nairobi, Kenya. He is speaking to the governments of both countries trying to get an idea of the disturbances in each country." Garland completed.

"Garland, what can I do?" Marko asked.

"You need to speak with your Boston Analysis Group (BAG), the Qatar Terrorist Analysis Group (Q-TAG) and Farimo or Adella."

"Well, I guess the honeymoon is over."

"Not necessarily, you probably have twenty-four hours before you must fly some where."

"I can't wait to tell Mei-Ling."

"Alright, I'll see you in New York," Garland hung-up the phone.

Marko shook his head and looked at the beautiful sea, waves gently rocking the boat and the sun bouncing off the water. He slowly went below to tell Mei-Ling. He reiterated the conversation with Garland and came to the part about the honeymoon being over.

Mei-Ling objected, "Honey, don't say that! This honeymoon will never be over no matter how long we are married!"

Mary Ann Peck has written non-fiction, scripts and been a member of the International Input-Output Association where she suggested they track the results of natural happenings, resulting in the Buenos Aires meeting covering that subject. The Velgrove Family will be seeing more action in the near future.

Russell C. Arslan a retired University economics professor with entrepreneurial portfolio is an internationalist bent on geopolitical and environmental issues. Just as importantly he is a storyteller that entertained you and stretches your awareness of your surroundings. Having traveled extensively to Asia, Central and South America, and Africa for more than five decades he brings his knowledge and experiences into his writings.

Books previously published
by Russell C. Arslan

Highest Stakes, "All In"

Matt Papaz's life began to change one morning when two Homeland Security Agents came to his gates and asked about an Armenian organization. Over the years he sent money to an Apostolic Church in Harpoots, Turkey called the Armenian Benevolent Union Church, but Homeland Security told him it was never a church, it's an Islamic Mosque and he is a person of interest because he has been supporting a terrorist network for twenty years. Despite the fact that he has no knowledge of the reality or the truth, he has to avoid possible charges of espionage and terrorism.

Those People

David Russell, traveling in Kenya with his two grown, adopted sons, was there to share his earlier life experiences with his boys. They had left Los Angeles on a trip that was to be a rite of passage. They encountered all his old friends and a new species in his search an example of his earlier life.

www.ingramcontent.com/pod-product-compliance
Lightning Source LLC
Chambersburg PA
CBHW070309260626
47160CB00003B/777